PATHS OF SEPARATIONS

Gulshan Ul Amin

authorHOUSE®

AuthorHouse™ UK Ltd.
1663 Liberty Drive
Bloomington, IN 47403 USA
www.authorhouse.co.uk
Phone: 0800.197.4150

Published by AuthorHouse   10/22/2013

ISBN: 978-1-4918-8266-5 (sc)
ISBN: 978-1-4918-8267-2 (e)

This is a work of fiction. All of the characters, names, incidents, organizations, and dialogue in this novel are either the products of the author's imagination or are used fictitiously.

Any people depicted in stock imagery provided by Thinkstock are models, and such images are being used for illustrative purposes only.
Certain stock imagery © Thinkstock.

This book is printed on acid-free paper.

Because of the dynamic nature of the Internet, any web addresses or links contained in this book may have changed since publication and may no longer be valid. The views expressed in this work are solely those of the author and do not necessarily reflect the views of the publisher, and the publisher hereby disclaims any responsibility for them.

PATHS OF SEPARATIONS

Contents

OCTOPUS

Jamal *Bhai* (brother), true to his words, had sent the sponsor letter. Whether Shabir would get the visa or not was up to his *kismet* (fate) now.

For years, Shabir had been pestering Jamal to call him over to England. Jamal, up till now, had successfully made excuses to keep him away from the idea. He had explained to Shabir that life in England was not as great and colourful as he imagined it to be. Every country had its ups and downs, goods and bads, advantages and disadvantages. England, he had explained, was a country like any other country, with its flaws and difficulties, and Shabir should stop living in dreams and vain hopes and should try to establish a solid foundation in the country of his origin. And in the end, Jamal had tried to put Shabir off by saying how difficult it was nowadays to obtain a British visa. But Shabir, as usual, had listened with one ear and thrown his elder brother's words out the other. To him, England was a country of great charm, opportunities, beauty, and wealth. Whoever went and settled there became automatically rich.

Last year, when Jamal had visited Pakistan, Shabir had emotionally blackmailed him, first by going out of his way to please him and second with a sad, worried look and telling him of the troublesome, depressing circumstances this country was going through. Poverty, corruption, disruption, bribery, and unemployment were affecting everyone. Educated people were forced to take lowly or low-paying jobs, and no one was safe nowadays, he said; everyone faced the risk of being robbed or blasted or gunned down. And all this happened in broad daylight. People were afraid to leave their houses, for the fear of never returning alive. Prices were rising day by day. Everything was so dear. No gas, no water, no electricity was made available to the public. Homes and businesses were suffering. And no sign of change seemed forthcoming either. Helplessness, constraints, and destruction were everywhere. There was no *izzat* (respect, honour) if you weren't rich or influential. And thirdly, he said with tears in his eyes, this person's brother did this for him and that person's brother did that for him. What kind of brother was Jamal? Here he was, Shabir living a shabby and miserable life, while he, Jamal was living a grand and wonderful life in England.

Jamal had looked at him then and had sighed as he shook his head in a resigned way. "You will never understand. All that glitters is not gold. And the grass is not always greener on the other side." He stood up. "I have tried my best to persuade you to stop living in Utopia."

Shabir had tried to say something, but Jamal had stopped him by raising his hand high.

"Yes, you do think of England as Utopia—a perfect land, where everyone's happy, comfortable, and carefree and living a life of enjoyment and pleasure. *Bhai mere*" (My brother), "this is not so . . . But, still, I will try to do whatever I can for you. I hate to think how disappointed you will be when you'll have to watch most of your colourful dreams turn into black and white. Now this is what you'll have to do . . ."

Shabir had all the important documents ready. Now Jamal had sent him the sponsor letter and a return air ticket, with a note saying, "I have done what I can. Take all these documents to the British Embassy. The rest is up to them and to your fate."

Shabir felt that he was flying in the air. He wanted to leave for the embassy straight away, but it was too late in the day for him to reach it in time. He'd have to wait till night.

He passed the day restlessly. His parents were unusually quiet. Earlier, when he had told his mother about the sponsor letter, she had gazed at him with an indefinable expression on her face and had asked, "You really want to go, don't you?"

Shabir had felt she was searching for something on his face, but he couldn't tell what. "Of course," he had replied enthusiastically. "You know it's one of the greatest aspirations of my life."

"Well, try it then. I pray that all your wishes will be fulfilled," she had said quietly.

His younger brother, Aslam, was as ardent as him, though, and was teasing him. "When you get to England, Shabir Bhai, don't forget to call me there too."

Shabir laughed and rumpled his hair fondly. "I have a hurdle to cross yet," he said, meaning the visa.

He wondered if he should tell Amna but then decided against it. He'd tell her when he got back from the embassy. Amna was funny about this subject. Every time he'd mentioned it, she had either changed it or avoided it or gone quiet. She just couldn't understand why Shabir had this urge to go to England. Shabir had tried explaining his motives for going—better life, better future, higher standard of living, good job, money, and so on. He wasn't just doing it for himself. He had the best of intentions in his heart, and he was concerned with the interests of everyone he cared for, most of all hers. She deserved a better life than the one she was leading. Shabir had hoped this would make her see his purpose for wanting to go.

Instead, she had given a little shrug and spread her hands. "But I don't mind this life. I'm used to it. I have been brought up this way. This has been our life for years."

"This is just it." He hit his fist furiously into the palm of his other hand. "You people are all like a frog in the well. You have no ambitions. You are content to live in your surroundings, with your own kind. You don't want to look beyond these four walls of your houses. You don't want to jump out of the well. You are satisfied, lying in your dark environment with only a little bit of sky for light. You people don't want to know that there is another world outside—a better, brighter world, with a full sky overhead, and I . . . "Shabir pointed his thumb resolutely at his chest. "I intend to have my share of that sky."

She was staring at him incredulously. "Is that what you really think of us?" Amusement was in her eyes now. Shabir had an uneasy feeling that she was laughing at him.

"Yes, I do." He stood up abruptly as if to leave, but he knew he wouldn't be able to leave. Amna was in his system, and he knew he couldn't get her out.

Suddenly, she grabbed his hand and smiled at him, which melted his heart and cooled his temper. "All right, Mr Rebellious Frog." There was a sparkle in her eyes. Tears? Shabir couldn't tell. Women were so unpredictable. "Before you jump out of this well, won't you stay to have some of my *mooli wale parathas*" (spicy reddish filled chapattis)?

He looked down at her. He couldn't be angry with her for long, especially when she was looking at him like that. He sat down.

5

Shabir left his home at about midnight and caught a direct night coach to Islamabad. Islamabad was a good four to five hours drive from where he lived. All the passengers in the coach were either sleeping or dozing. He was too excited to sleep. He wondered whether or not he would be granted a visa. He had heard many stories regarding the visa. If you were lucky and the *goras* (white or English men) were satisfied, they would give you a visa on the same day. If you weren't lucky and the goras were not satisfied, they refused you there and then. Sometimes they gave you a date to come back again. He knew of so many cases where a person was given date after date, for an application, either to be accepted or rejected. He wondered, with a thumping heart, what would happen to him. Quickly, he started reciting all the prayers he knew.

Ya Allah! Khair kari" (O Allah, do well)." He kept repeating silently.

At about 5.00 a.m., the coach stopped at its destination. Shabir got off and stretched his aching back and cramped legs. He refreshed himself at a roadside cafe and then took a taxi to the British Embassy. He had thought that he was early but was surprised to find a long queue of people at the door of the embassy (which wasn't open yet).

It seemed to Shabir that the whole of the country wanted to go to England. People from various parts of the country and walks of life were lined up for that purpose. He joined the ever-increasing queue. The weather was getting extremely hot and Shabir was already sweaty. The man in front of Shabir smelt of perspiration. Every time he moved, the sour smell would drift into Shabir's nostrils. The man behind Shabir was chewing *paan* (betel leaf). Every time he spat out the red saliva, Shabir would jump away to save his clothes from being coloured.

The door of the embassy finally opened, and every person was checked before being allowed to enter. Shabir went to his required section, paid his visa fee, and handed his papers to a gora (white, English) officer standing behind the reception counter. The gora checked Shabir's papers and asked, "Can you understand English?"

Though Shabir had always prided himself on his English, he found it hard to understand the accent.

The gora repeated his question again, but slowly this time.

"A little bit," said Shabir, smiling foolishly at the gora. Just the sight of a white man was enough to make Shabir's knees shake, *What will I be asked?* His heart fluttered.

"Why do you want to go to England?"

Shabir could hardly comprehend what the gora was saying. He cursed his English, which he had thought so brilliant.

"To . . . visit . . . my brother," he managed to say haltingly.

The gora gathered up the papers, clipped them, and said, "Okay, you can sit down and wait for your turn to be called in for an interview."

Shabir sat down and looked around. The room was crowded with "visa wishers". Here were the young, the old, the middle aged, the single, and the married, some with children and some without. Here were the the the city people, the villagers, the literates and the illiterates. Here were the poor, the wealthy and the not so wealthy. They were all there, with the same apprehensive look in their eyes and on their faces. Would they get the magical visa? Of course there were the confident ones too, like that big fat businessman over there, who sat reading the newspaper as though he hadn't a care in the world. And there were the nervous ones, like the students in the third row nervously twitching their shoulders.

The calls for the interview had begun. One by one, each person or family was called into one of the interview rooms. Shabir studied each person as he or she or they went in and as he or she or they came out. The ones who had been granted visas came out smiling. The ones who had been refused came out looking dejected, despair showing plainly on their faces. The ones who had been given dates came out with the same confused look they'd worn as they'd gone in for the interview.

"This is my fourth attempt," the man next to Shabir was grumbling. "It's been ages since I've been coming here. And I have to come from so far. Still these gorés have no pity on me. I've had enough, I tell you. This is the last time I'm going to try. If they give me a visa this time . . . fine. If they don't I'm going to write to my brother, who's trying to call me there, to stuff his England." He swore and spat on the floor.

Shabir thought *What if this should happen to me?* His heart sank.

A family of five was coming out from behind the reception counter where the interview rooms were located, with joyous expressions on their faces. Their application had been successful. They were a peasant family from a certain underdeveloped, rural part of the country. A thick air of peasantness surrounded them, which would remain with them for the rest of their lives, no matter where they lived or what they did. The man was scruffy, his *shalwar kameez* (Pakistan's traditional and national dress worn by both men and women, loose trousers (shalwar), a long shirt or tunic (kameez) was dirty and crumpled. His oiled hair was plastered to his head. The woman was covered in a black *burkha* and she had red socks and golden sandals on her feet. She had rubbed her teeth with *sak* (the bark of a certain tree), which had coloured her lips and gums dark red. The three children were dressed in oversized clothes and *chapals* (sandals). Their feet and nails were covered with permanent dirt. Their hair was closely cropped, and like their father, they too had poured heaps of mustard oil on their head.

"*Gande pendoos*" (dirty villagers or village idiots), muttered the man next to Shabir. "These people, always get their visas instantly." The man gave the family a loathsome look. Grinning like simpletons from ear to ear, shouting *vekhao, vekhao* (let's have a look), to each other and trying to snatch the passports from each other's hand to gaze at the visa in wonder the peasant family made their way out.

An old man, wearing a shirt, a white *dhoti* (a piece of cloth wrapped around his waist) and a white *pag* (turban) on his head, was coming out slowly from his interview. His hand on the top of his walking stick was shaking with indignation. He was weeping loudly and swearing openly. His young companion, who had been waiting outside, stood up to comfort him.

"*Soor ke bache*" (Children of pigs), the old man cried. "Refusing me a visa. I only want to see my son and my grandchildren. I haven't seen them for years. These gorés are supposed to be fair people. Where is the fairness in this, denying an old man the last wish and joy of his lifetime? Oh, my grandchildren, how disappointed they will be that their grandfather cannot come to England to see them," he wailed.

"*O Baba Ji, chup kar jao*" (Old man, be quiet)," the man next to Shabir called out. "Go home and wait for your visa to arrive from the next world."

The stick the old man was holding fell to the floor, and in a flash, he grabbed the man next to Shabir by the collar. "I'll tell you . . . talking to me like that. I'll . . ." The old man's voice choked with rage. Spit was gathering at the corner of his mouth. His young companion held him with both hands and pulled him away firmly.

"Come on, Baba Ji. Let's go home. What's the use of making a spectacle of yourself here?" The young companion bent down and picked the stick up from the floor. "What did they say?" he asked, handing the stick back to the old man.

"They said one of my papers was not the right one." The old man wept, taking the stick.

"Well, they haven't refused you then, have they? We will inform your son in England, and as soon as he sends you the right paper, you'll be off to see your grandchildren." The young companion laid a comforting hand on the old man's arm.

The old man's face brightened. "Well, the gora officer did say I didn't have to come to the embassy again. I could just post it to them."

"There you are then. They are fair. You see, they have to have the correct papers. Mark my word. You'll get your visa while sitting at home," the young companion said as he led the old man out of the waiting room.

The man next to Shabir shrugged his shoulders and straightened his collar. "*Pagal budдha*" (Stupid old man), "taking his anger out on me. Why, he should be hitting the gora not me." He sat down again.

A fashionable woman was coming out from her interview, clutching her purse. She was wearing a blouse and trousers. She too had been refused a visa. She tried to appear cheerful, but Shabir could see her eyes were watery, her eyeliner smudged, and the powder on her face was cracking as surely her heart was.

"I didn't really want to go," she was saying to someone. "I couldn't care less about England. What is there? Nothing. I have everything here—everything I could ever want. I wouldn't even look at England." She went out, her high heels tapping on the chipped floor.

The man beside Shabir laughed sarcastically. "Liar. Hypocrite. Double faced bitch. She's desperate to go—anywhere . . . out of Pakistan. She's been trying at the American, the French, even the Japanese Embassy."

Shabir remembered that, earlier, this woman had been sitting in front of him, and he had overheard her saying to someone while she had been delicately fanning herself with a piece of paper, "I'm dying to go to England. Oh, the life there—the freedom. You can do anything you want to do, wear anything you want to. No one to stare at you. No restrictions whatsoever. What is here in Pakistan? Nothing but heat, dirt, flies, mosquitoes . . . and don't do this and don't do that . . ."

The big fat businessman came out cool and confident, looking haughty and careless.

"*Saalaa*" (a sort of swear word) *chakar baaz*" (fraudster, black marketer). He'll always get a visa. He has *lambé haath*" (long hands). They reach everywhere," the man next to Shabir snorted in disdain.

Shabir wondered how the man knew everything about everybody. It seemed he had lived a life in the embassy.

12

The students were back from their interviews. Two of them had radiant expressions on their faces. They were off to a new land, with big dreams in their eyes and high hopes in their hearts. The third one looked dejected.

"Oh, cheer up, *yaar*" (friend)," the one with the visa said. "You haven't been rejected. You've been given a date. You are sure to get it on the next date." The two happy students comforted their third distressed friend as they all went towards the exit door.

"He'll probably get it next time," the man next to Shabir said. "These students"—he shook his head sideways and clicked his tongue—"their heads are filled with big ideas and dreams. They dream of the day when they'll be called 'England Returns' or 'Educated from England', but you know what will happen? They will never return."

Shabir's attention was caught by a distraught looking young man of his age, who was coming from his interview, his green Pakistani passport sticking out of his shirt pocket. He ran his hand despairingly over his already ruffled hair. He looked disoriented and unhappy. It was distinctly obvious he had been refused a visa. Shabir's heart shook. He didn't want that to happen to him. His saddened eyes followed the crestfallen disappointed young man's back as he walked towards the outer door.

"I'm telling you; these students will never return," the man next to Shabir repeated, oblivious to Shabir's inattentiveness and agitated state.

The young man had walked out of the exit door, shoulders hunched, head bowed. Shabir's eyes returned to the waiting room. He felt downhearted.

The man next to Shabir was saying knowingly, "Oh, yes, they'll be homesick and lonely at first, in a strange land, strange people and strange culture, but with passing time they'll be so influenced by the Western culture that they will look down upon the country of their birth. They will behave as if they had always belonged in and to England. And when they get their degrees, instead of returning as they had once longed for, they'll prefer to stay and work in that country, and they'll eventually marry there, probably a *gori*" (white woman). "They will forget that their mothers had sold their gold jewellery, their last possession, to pay for their fare and education fees. They will forget that their fathers had laboured and toiled all their lives, had skimped and saved to send them to schools and colleges. They will forget that their grown-up sisters will watch their *raste*" (ways, paths) and their hearts will break a thousand times when their brothers won't be there to give shoulders to their *dolis*" (marriage palanquin in which the bride is carried by her brothers and cousin brothers for a short distance)." The man turned towards Shabir. "Tell me," he asked, "tell me who plants a tree and who eats the fruit?"

Shabir was getting fed up with the man's non-stop talking. He looked around to change his seat.

"I'll tell you," the man said undisturbed by Shabir's annoyance. "The parents plant a tree, save it from sun and rain, nourish it with their sweat and blood, and when the time comes for them to reap the fruit, they find that the fruit has fallen into someone else's lap. And if, after much pleading and imploring from their old parents, these students—they'll be husbands and fathers by then—will ever visit the country of their birth, they'll be embarrassed of their mothers, with holes in their *dupattas*" (long scarves or stoles that go with women's shalwar kameezes), "and the smell of onions and ghee coming from them will disgust them. They will prefer to forget that they had been brought up with that smell. They will recoil at the sight of their shrivelled old work-weary fathers. And they will be relieved to get back to England."

Shabir felt he would scream if the man didn't stop. His hands itched to hit the man in the face. Why wouldn't the man shut up?

The man continued, unaware of Shabir's agony, "And when their sons will ask them, 'Dad, am I English or Pakistani?' the mother will reply hurriedly, 'English, of course.' And when their daughters will come home someday and say, 'Dad, meet my boyfriend,' the roots in their hearts, which they had forcefully sent to sleep, will start awakening from their slumber and will start squeezing their heart, but by then, it will be too late."

Shabir felt like tearing his own hair out. His hand curled and uncurled in his lap. He wanted to seize the man by the neck and throttle him.

"You see," said the man, fixing his gaze on Shabir, "that country is like an octopus. It will grab you with its tentacles and won't release you until it takes the last breath out of you."

Shabir got up; made fists with his hands; and, with eyes blazing, moved fiercely towards the man. He was going to take the breath out of this man.

"Ah," said the man. "Ah, I can see you don't like reality, but it happens. Cool yourself . . . because your name's going to be announced any minute now."

Shabir's fist was left suspended in mid-air. As the man had predicted, his name was indeed being called out for the interview. He glared at the man as he lowered his fist.

"Well," called out the man as Shabir made his way to the interview room, "good luck. Look, if you are really desperate for this visa, take a tip from me. Lie. Lie a lot. Don't speak the truth whatever you do. Look where it got me. It never does well to speak the truth with a gora. They are prejudiced. They will do everything to discourage you. Tell them you have heaps of money. Tell them you are a big businessman. Tell them you'll convert all your business to England. Tell them you'll . . ." His voice faded.

Shabir entered the interview room with hope, fear, and confusion filling his heart. The gora officer was sitting on a chair, with Shabir's papers on the table in front of him. A woman interpreter was standing on one side. She smiled politely at him. Shabir wondered if he ought to shake hands with the gora.

"Please, take a seat," said the gora, giving him a customary nod. Shabir sat down opposite the gora and folded his hands tightly under the table to stop them from shaking. He felt nervous and tensed up, and he knew it showed.

"Do you need an interpreter?" asked the gora.

Shabir decided at once that he did. He would feel better talking in his own language.

The general questions began. Name? Address? Occupation? Age? Marital status? Name, address, occupation of Jamal? His wife's name? His number of children, their names and ages? The cross questioning was beginning now. How many brothers and sisters did he have? Who did he live with? Who would provide for his parents while he was gone? Had he ever visited England before? Had he ever applied for a visa for another European country before? Why had Jamal sent him the ticket? Was it because he couldn't afford it himself?

The interrogation was getting harder.

Shabir's lips and throat were dry. Time dragged by. He felt sick and tired and wished for the interview to be over.

The gora was asking him his reason for visiting London.

"To . . . see . . . my brother," Shabir said, his heart fluttering. Obviously, he wanted to add but refrained himself.

"When did you last see your brother?"

"About six months ago."

"About six months ago!" repeated the gora. "And you want to see him so soon again. Why?"

Shabir looked nervously at the gora's face. This was a very tricky question. What should he say? The gora was watching him closely. Should he lie? Should he say something like Jamal was ill, his wife was ill, one of the children was ill?

"Well," he cleared his throat. "I just want . . ." He faltered. "I just want to visit my brother . . . to see my nephews and niece . . . . I just want to see England . . . for holidays. I won't be staying there . . ." He knew he was babbling and that he should stop. He might say something to make the gora suspicious of his motives for going to England. Of course, once he got the visa, he had no attention of coming back, for good that was.

"What arrangements have you made for staying in London if you were to be granted a visa?"

"I'll stay with my brother."

"Is your brother capable of putting you up through your stay?"

"Oh, yes," said Shabir quickly—too quickly. He must keep calm. "He owns a house. He works. He earns good . . . I'll be taking some of my own money too." He really must stop. He didn't want the gora to have any doubts.

"How long do you want the visa for?" The gora fixed his eyes on Shabir.

Shabir went into a flutter. Was he going to get the visa after all? *For life, you fool*, he wanted to shout. But he knew he must keep his senses. One wrong word and he could be finished.

"I . . . I don't know. A month . . . perhaps two months" *Any extent will do. I just need to enter Britain. I'll find a way to stay there permanently. Just grant me a visa*, his heart screamed. *Hurry up.*

The gora was gathering up the papers. "Well, Mr Shabir."

Shabir held his breath. His whole future depended on the gora's decision. He listened with his heart in his mouth. This moment could break him or make him.

"I'll grant you a visa for six months. No more. You must come back within this period."

"Oh yes, yes. I will," Shabir said, greatly relieved. *Oh no, I won't*, Shabir's heart said joyously.

"Please wait here while I have your visa stamped on your passport." The gora left the room with the interpreter.

Shabir tried to calm his thumping heart. A miracle, yes, a miracle had happened. His prayers had been answered. He had gotten the magical visa. He wanted to jump from the chair and fall on his knees and lie prostrate to thank Allah

He came out of the interview room, starry-eyed and dazed, his passport and ticket clutched to his heart. The waiting room was almost empty now. The few expectants left were watching him with eager interest, trying to judge by his expression whether it had been a yes or a no.

He left the embassy feeling light-hearted. He wanted to hop, skip, and shout with delight. And while he was standing by the roadside, waiting for a taxi, he thought of the man at the embassy, sitting next to him. He wondered whether the man had been granted a visa on his fourth attempt.

Shabir reached home with his head in the clouds. In his imagination, he was already travelling to England. As soon as he entered the yard of his house, he gave a jubilant shout.

"I've got it. I've got the visa for England." He waved the passport over his head.

Aslam, who was eagerly awaiting his return, reached him first and danced around him. "Let's have a look. Ha, ha, we are going to England."

"Not we, but me." Shabir was all smiles.

His mother hurried out of the kitchen, wiping her hands on her dupatta. Shabir bowed his head in a gesture of respect as she came near him. Gently and lovingly, she stroked his head with her hand and kissed him on the forehead. Tears fell softly from her eyes as she said with a trembling voice, *"mera pardesi putre"* (my foreigner son) . . . *Mera doosra pardesi putre"* (my second foreigner son)."

His father, who was sitting on the *charpoy* (roped bed with wooden rods frame) smoking his hookah, made an attempt to get up.

Shabir rushed to him. "*Aba Ji*" (Father), "look . . . visa." He held out the open passport page with the visa stamp to the old man.

The man looked at it and said, "I'm happy for you. Congratulations, son." His voice was tinged with sorrow—sorrow for the now inevitable separation from his son. He put the hookah's mouthpiece back in his mouth and puffed and drew on it, trying to drown his sorrow in the gurgle of the hookah's water pot.

Shabir had already phoned Jamal from the telephone exchange at Islamabad. Now he went to phone his two sisters from one of the neighbour's house, as he didn't have a phone at his own house. The neighbours stared at him as if he had grown two horns, and in disbelief at his good luck, when he told them about receiving the visa. He phoned his sisters. They screamed and shrieked their delight into the receiver. His brothers-in-law congratulated him and joked that soon he would be joining the goras in goraland (white people's land).

He told his friends, and they said enviously, "You lucky devil. How did you do it? They don't usually give visas to young men."

And then he went to see **Amna**. She was sitting as usual in her favourite place, in the further end of her house's yard, on a *peerhi* (a low stool made of ropes with wooden frames), in front of the clay hearth. She was making senseless, oblique lines with a piece of coal on the bricked floor.

She looked at his radiant face as he entered and said, "So you've got it. Your wish has come true."

He pulled another peerhi beside her.

"Yes. Oh, Amna, I'm so happy."

"I can see that." Her dupatta had slipped from her head and was lying loosely around her shoulders.

"Aren't you happy?"

She lowered her head. Her voice shook as she said, "Of course I am. Congratulations. So . . ." she paused for a moment but still didn't look up—"when are you going?"

"Amna, Amna, are you crying?" Shabir held her head with both of his hands and forced it up. Her eyes were closed and tears were sliding down her cheeks.

"No." She sniffed. "I'm not crying. It's just that smoke got in my eyes."

"Look at me, Amna. Listen to me," Shabir beseeched, his heart aching. "I'm doing this for you too."

"For me?" Her eyes flew open. "For me, Shabir? Oh, come off it. When did I ask you to do this for me?"

She hadn't. Ever.

"Well, whatever I do concerns you too, doesn't it?" His voice was rough with emotions. "Your dreams and my dreams cannot be separated."

"This is not my dream, Shabir. This is your dream. Only yours. Tell me, what's wrong with living here? Don't people survive here? Don't they eat, breath, and live?"

"Yes, they do, but we are not talking about other people. We are talking about ourselves. I want to give you a good life, a better life. I hate it when I see you washing ugly silver utensils with ashes. I hate it when I see you rubbing home-made soap on the wet clothes and then beating them with a stick to get the dirt out. I hate it when I see you pumping water from the hand pump for your every use. I hate it when I see you blow on dry sticks to light the fire in the hearth. I want to see you, Amna, in a modern-fitted kitchen, with shining pots and pans bubbling on a gas cooker, the dirty linen in the washing machine, and sinks with mixer taps to give you hot and cold water whenever you need it." He touched her arms. "I want to fill your arms with gold bangles, and I want you to wear fine clothes. I want you to travel in cars. I dislike seeing you standing in the street waiting for a *tonga*" (horse cart for passengers) "or a *racksha*" (rickshaw) "if you want to go somewhere. Isn't it my right to dream of a good life for you?"

Amna looked at him intently. "Has it ever occurred to you that I might not want all this?"

It had; it had occurred to Shabir a hundred times. He knew Amna wasn't a material girl.

"Not if it's going to separate you from me. I can't bear your separation. I can't." Her eyes were bright with tears.

"Listen, Amna," Shabir said, his heart full. He held her face between both of his hands. "I love you. I always have, and I always will. But this dream has been with

23

me for so long, and now the time has come for it to be fulfilled. Please don't spoil it," he pleaded.

Amna wiped her eyes with her dupatta and placed it back on her head. She lowered her gaze. "Will you have some tea?" She poked a stick into the clay stove and searched for a spark in the ashes. She shoved some more sticks in and blew hard. The fire lit up. She put some water from a nearby jug, which she had filled earlier from the hand pump, in a much-used dented silver pan and placed it on the clay hearth. She added some tea leaves and milk and let it boil. Soon the tea was ready.

The day of departure had arrived. The house was full of relatives, friends, and neighbours. They had all gathered to see Shabir off. The atmosphere was of mixed emotions. Laughter mingled with tears. Sadness hugged happiness, and lips trembled as they spoke. Aslam was reminding him over and over again, "Shabir Bhai, don't forget me when you get there. Do something for me to call me over too."

His brothers-in-law were joking, "We've heard that there are many beautiful attractions to distract a mind. Amna should be warned."

His sisters too were laughing and teasing him about England, about Amna, and about the pretty goris there. They had brought presents for him, for Jamal Bhai, Sara *Bhabi* (brother's wife (bhabi), and their children. His mother had also made some *achaars* (pickles), chutneys, and handmade vermicelli.

Shabir looked at the door again. Still Amna or her parents hadn't arrived. Time was running short. Where was she? He went impatiently towards the front door and glanced at the street. Amna's father was coming alone.

"*Aslaam O Alaikum*" (Muslim greetings, salutations, peace be upon you), "*Chacha*" (Uncle). "What took you so long? Why isn't Amna with you?"

"*Wa Alaikum Salaam*" (peace be upon you, standard response to the greeting *Aslaam O Alaikum*). *beta*" (son, also daughter or child), "sorry for being a bit late. I just had some little things to do."

"And Amna? And *Chachi*" (Aunty), "are they on their way here?" Shabir's voice was anxious.

Amna's father avoided Shabir's eyes. "They are still at home—Ah . . . I can see your father calling me. Excuse me." He went off hurriedly.

Shabir gazed at the man's back with bewilderment. His mother saw the look on his face. She too had seen Amna's father arrive by himself. She came over to Shabir and gently laid a hand on his arm.

"If I were you I'd go over and see what's happened."

Shabir looked at her with respect. She always could read him clearly.

A strange silence hung over Amna's street and house. Her mother was breaking a dry *roti* (chapatti) into small pieces for her pet chickens to feed when he stepped into the yard.

"*Salaam,*"(hello, greetings, peace upon you) Chachi." He bowed his head in front of her in a gesture of respect.

She stroked his head and said, "*Wa Salaam*", (peace upon you, standard response to Salaam). "*Jeete raho*" (Live long).

"I will be leaving soon. Why haven't you and Amna come over to the house yet?"

She regarded Shabir sadly.

"I wanted to, beté, but Amna . . ."

Shabir's heart nearly stopped beating.

"What's happened to Amna?" Shabir was panicking.

"No. Nothing's happened, but . . ."

"For God's sake, Chachi, hurry up and tell me, or I'll go crazy."

"She's been strange since this morning. Understandably, of course. I have begged her to come with me to your house, but she's refused. I couldn't leave her by herself, now could I?"

"Where is she?" Shabir asked.

"She's inside. Go and speak some words of comfort to her. She needs your consolation."

As Shabir went towards the room, he passed Amna's favourite place. Her peerhi was still there by the clay stove. His heart filled with pain. He and Amna had spent many beautiful moments here, and he was leaving all this for some unknown and unseen land.

Amna was sitting on the charpoy staring at the floor. She looked up when she sensed Shabir in the doorway. Shabir's heart went out to her. She looked so lost and forlorn. He went to her.

"I'll be leaving soon. Why haven't you come to the house?"

"How cruel can you be? First you give me wounds, and now you have come to rub salt in them. You know I can't watch you go. I don't possess the kind of strength that you do."

Shabir felt his heart breaking. How dear, sweet, and simple she was in expressing herself.

"Amna, Amna darling, listen to me. I'm doing this for you too. I'm—"

"Stop." She stood up. "Quit these dialogues. Don't make excuses for going. Don't you see that I don't want all this? All I want is your love, your affection, your companionship. I want you to stay with me—to live on whatever this country has to offer us. I'll eat plain roti. I'll drink plain water. As long as we are together, nothing else matters." The tears that she had kept stored in her eyes were falling now.

All sorts of emotions were tangled inside Shabir. He made a move towards her. "You are my kismet, Amna. And we will be together one day, I promise you."

"Kismets are too strong, too powerful for us human beings. No one ever knows where their kismet will lead them to."

"Nothing can come between us," he insisted.

She laughed bitterly. "Oh, but it already has, Shabir. A country has come between us. It's taking you away from me. Its fascination is too much for a young man like you to resist. You are intoxicated by it."

"I'm intoxicated by you too. You are in my system."

"Yes, but you can bring yourself out of my intoxication whenever you want. The other intoxication has a hold on you, much stronger than my intoxication, and I'm afraid that it will win you."

"Why are you talking like this to me?" he said wretchedly. "I will come back and marry you . . . and take you with me." He reached out and pulled her close to him. "You will wait for me?" A lump rose in Shabir's throat.

"I will wait, Shabir, but will you come back? Will you?"

She pulled at his shirt hysterically. Shabir's own heart felt as though it would burst. He held her tightly in his arms, as she sobbed wildly. After a while, she calmed down and disengaged herself from him.

"I am sorry." She sniffed. "You are going so far away, and I've upset you. You know I've always been emotional and silly."

"You have always been dear and lovely and always will be." Shabir's voice was thick with emotions. She moved away from him, and his hands fell to his side.

"You should be going now; otherwise, you'll miss your flight." She stood in front of him, her eyes downcast.

Shabir looked at her, taking in his heart her every feature, her every gesture, and still looking at her, he slowly took a step backwards. Then tearing himself away, he abruptly swung himself out of the door.

Amna's mother was still in the yard, feeding her chickens.

"Ah, ah, ah, ah," she called out to the chickens as she threw the pieces of roti on the floor for them to eat.

"Okay, Chachi. This is goodbye from me." "Beté," said Amna's mother, "before you go, there is something I would like to say to you. Amna's present age is suitable for marriage. It would have been better if you had stayed here and married her, or you should have married her and taken her with you. But seeing your aspirations we, me and Amna's father, did not want to force you or stand in your way. Just remember, a young daughter of a marriageable age is a burden to her parents. Though the parents love and cherish this burden, they still long for someone worthy to lift it off their shoulders. This is all I want to say. Go now. You have our blessings with you."

Heathrow Airport.

Shabir had read about it, and now here he was, about to take his first step into the worlds busiest and most famous airport.

"*Bissmillah irrehmanirrahim*" (In the name of Allah, The Most Gracious, The Most Merciful), he said very quietly as he stepped down from the plane.

He had informed Jamal Bhai the time of the arrival of his flight. Jamal had assured him he would be there with his family and all the necessary paperwork to receive him. If he had any trouble with the entry clearance, the passport control officials would announce for him, Jamal, and he would be there to support him. But Shabir had no problems with the entry, and soon after collecting his luggage, he came out of the arrivals, his heart thudding.

Yes, Jamal Bhai was there, embracing him warmly. Sara Bhabi too hugged him, asking how he was. And their three children, one by one, came forward to greet and hug their uncle. Maybe he was imagining it, but Shabir sensed that Sara Bhabi was a bit aloof—not as pleased as he had imagined she would be at seeing him.

He shrugged his doubts away as they packed into Jamal Bhai's car. Jamal sat in the driver's seat, with Sara next to him. Shabir sat in the back with the children. He thought, *if I had Amna with me in the car, I would have let Jamal Bhai sit in the front, and Amna, out of respect, would have sat in the back.* Then he chuckled at his own typical Pakistani mentality and reminded himself that this was England, where women were equal to men. If offering the front seat to their husband's relatives made these British Asian women less respectable, then good luck to them. They could keep their seat.

He forgot everything as he got his first glimpse of England. How he had longed for this country. He had come here with hopes of bettering his prospects. Would this country be harsh or kind to him? Would it welcome him? He hoped so.

Jamal was steering through London's busy traffic now.

London—depicting glories past and present. A city of bright lights and wonderment. A city of millions of people of diverse cultures, rich in history and traditions.

As Jamal drove, he enquired after their parents, the rest of the family, and relatives. He asked about Pakistan, its reforms and present circumstances.

Shabir answered with as much attention he could pay. He was too busy looking at the buildings that sped by. London didn't look as picturesque or as beautiful as it did in the postcards and pictures. In fact, some of the buildings looked downright gloomy and grey, and there was a sense of confinement, closeness about them.

But there were colourful people on the streets. London had absorbed people from all over the world. Shabir had never seen so many people of different races, colours, cultures, and religions. He wondered if any "pure" English people remained among the sea of foreigners and mixed races.

He looked interestedly out of the car window. A black man was walking on the footpath. In Pakistan, everyone would have stopped and stared at him and his colour, but here no one paid any notice to his black colour, his flat nose and thick lips, and his wiry hair.

And the black man was wearing a suit and holding a briefcase—a black businessman. *Well, why not?* thought Shabir. They are people just like us.

And look at those two Asian girls—Indian or Pakistani, he couldn't tell—wearing jeans and short tops with bags slung over their shoulders. Two young Asian boys had just joined them. Their baggy trousers were worn so low and so loose that it seemed one little pull would cause the trousers to fall to the ground. Shabir almost laughed out loud at this thought. The foursome were talking and laughing together. Every now and then one would throw his or her hand, palm down, on the outstretched hand, palm up, of the other, playfully, while they laughed and joked. In Pakistan, this kind of behaviour, girls and boys mixing together so closely, would have been seen as a disgrace. People would have called these girls "fast", "clever", "*badmaashnian*" (loose, bad girls), and God knows what else.

The car sped on. Shabir looked back from the rear window. Yes, the four young people were still there, standing there laughing and joking together, and no one cared. No one even looked in their direction.

An Arab wearing a long white loose shirt, with a white and red checked scarf held by a black round band on his head, was walking with a very fancy lady, perhaps his wife. The lady was plump and very made up. She was wearing a long black embroidered dress and was adorned all over with gold jewellery. Some rich sheikhs probably.

The car stopped at traffic lights. A gori was coming out of the newsagents'. My God, what was she wearing? A tight-fitting black miniskirt and a skimpy sleeveless top; it barely covered her stomach. And she was not ashamed to show her long white legs and white arms. And she was quite beautiful too. Shabir stared at her for a while and then laughed at himself. *Shabir beté, you'd better get used to all this. You will find hundreds of attractive distractions like this on every corner here. You can't stop and stare at each one of them.*

Jamal Bhai turned the car into a residential street and parked it on the road near the kerb. Rows of houses lined each side of the street. A woman wearing shalwar kameez was in her front garden, throwing a black bag of rubbish into the bin. She gave them a strange look and then went inside. Shabir thought that, if they'd been in Pakistan, the whole neighbourhood would have gathered around him to greet him.

Jamal Bhai had started taking the luggage out of the car. Shabir hurried to help him. Sara Bhabi had walked to a house and was unlocking the door.

"Well," said Jamal Bhai, turning towards Shabir, "this is it. This is my street and that's my house."

Both of the brothers picked up the luggage and made their way to the house. There it was. Number 32. Shabir had sent many letters to this address. He mouthed "*Bissmillha*" (In the name of Allah) and stepped inside.

Shabir didn't know what to make of the house. It reminded him of a box, but he was careful not to say anything. He didn't want to appear gauche or ignorant. Jamal Bhai was clearly proud of his house.

"You want to look around the house first, or are you too tired?" he asked.

"Oh no, please, let's have a look at the house first," Shabir said eagerly.

"Right then. This is the through lounge, where you are now. Actually it was two reception rooms, but I had this wall taken out"—he pointed at the place where a wall had been—"and now I have a large sitting and dining room together. And I had it decorated recently— new carpets, new lights, new wall paper, etc. etc."

"Very nice," said Shabir. He had only heard of or seen carpeted and wallpapered houses in magazines.

Jamal Bhai was in the passage now. He walked to an open door at the end of the passage. "This is the kitchen."

Shabir could see that it was all very modernly fitted, but it was very small. He wondered how Sara Bhabi managed to cook for huge family gatherings or friends.

Jamal Bhai led him up the stairs. The stairs heaved and creaked with each step. Upstairs were three bedrooms. The master bedroom belonged to Jamal Bhai and Sara Bhabi. Shabir saw a sewing machine by the window. Plastic bags filled with unsewn materials were on the floor by the machine. The second bedroom belonged to the two boys, Usman and Bilal. Shabir looked in. He saw two single beds on each side, a desk in between them, and a wardrobe at the end of one bed. There was hardly any space for anything else. The third bedroom was a box room—Nazia's room. It contained a single bed, a tall narrow wardrobe, and a small dressing table. Shabir wondered where he would sleep.

"And this is the bathroom." Jamal Bhai proudly flung open a door. The bathroom was shining and clean. "I've just had it recently done. Isn't it beautiful?" Jamal Bhai looked at Shabir, waiting to hear words of praise. The bathroom was indeed beautiful. Fully tiled. Taps gleaming. Matching lino on the floor.

"Yes, it is," agreed Shabir, eyeing the toilet. He would have to get used to these toilets. He had already experienced one on the plane. If he could manage that, then he certainly could this one.

After supper, Shabir opened his suitcase and handed out the presents his mother and sisters had sent for Sara Bhabi and the children. Once again, he sensed Sara Bhabi's lack of interest. He quickly dismissed what he read in her demeanour from his mind. He wasn't here to bear any grudges against anyone, certainly not Sara Bhabi. She had a place of respect in his heart.

The problem of Shabir's sleeping, which had been in Shabir's mind for a while now, was solved in a flick of finger.

Jamal Bhai said, "This is where you'll sleep." He pointed at a sofa, with a teasing look on his face. He watched Shabir's face for a moment and then laughed.

"You idiot." He said hitting him lovingly on the shoulder. "I know you won't be able to sleep on the sofa. Look, this is a folding sofa bed." He pulled the sofa out a little bit and then pushed the back down, and Shabir saw that it had turned into a bed.

"You can keep your things in the cupboard on the landing. I've cleared it for you."

So this was how Shabir's sleeping arrangement was made. He didn't mind at all, as he had mentally prepared himself to pass through any kind of situation. He was ready to struggle, walk on rough paths, do any kind of work, and tackle any problems that came his way. He was here to make something of his life, and that he would do.

For the first few days, Shabir explored the area. He walked around the high street, looking at shops inside and outside. Most shops and restaurants were run by Asians. It seemed to be their favourite business. He was pleasantly surprised to find people conversing in their own mother tongues. The area had its own local church, *gurdwara* (Sikh worship place), *mandir* (Hindu worship place), and a *masjid* (mosque, Muslim worship place).

He took the children—Usman, Bilal, and Nazia—to school and collected them when it was time for them to come home. He helped Sara Bhabi with her shopping. He watched amusedly at people pushing their shopping trolleys and then standing in a queue to pay at the counter.

Once, he sat on those famous red double decker buses. Jamal Bhai had explained to him how to pay the conductor. He'd been thoroughly pleased with himself when he had managed to climb the stairs to the upper deck, while the bus was moving.

And while he wandered around, he thought and pondered over what he could do while he was here. He knew his visa was for six months, but he didn't give that a much thought. Stay he would. Of that, he had no doubt.

But in spite of his intentions to stay, he missed his homeland. He never realised how much he would do so. He felt lonely and homesick. He missed his mother. He remembered her face as she had hugged him and kissed his forehead when she had bid him goodbye. She had looked at him as though for the last time. He missed his father. He remembered how the older man's hand had shaken as he had placed it on his head to give him his blessings and said, "*Allah Hafiz, mere beté*" (goodbye, may Allah protect you, my son)." Shabir had realised with a shock then how old his father had really looked. Hard work all his life had taken its toil on him. He missed Aslam's wittiness and mischievousness.

And most of all he missed Amna. She was everywhere with him—in his eyes, in his heart, in his mind, in every breath he took. There would come a day when they would be together. He would give her life's luxuries. She deserved the best.

Jamal Bhai was a supervisor in a garment factory. He would leave for work every morning and be back in the evening. At night, the brothers would discuss the possibilities of Shabir's permanent stay.

"How about political asylum?" Shabir asked.

Jamal Bhai rejected the idea at once. "Too much of a hassle," he said, shaking his head. "The lawyers, the fees, the dates, the comings and goings to the Home Office, and the fear that's inside you, never knowing for sure whether or not you will be granted an indefinite leave. The procedure can take ages. You'll be hanging on tenterhooks. You won't be permitted to work, not openly anyway. You don't want to live on benefits all your life, *yaar*" (friend or pal). "I know some people actually enjoy that living, but I don't call that a life. Naa, yaar, forget it."

One night, after Sara and the children had gone to bed, Jamal told Shabir about his life when he had first come to England.

"The lure of London and its opportunities had been a significant factor in my decision to leave Pakistan," he began. "When I came to London, I had no relatives or friends to support me. People coming nowadays are lucky. They already have well-settled relatives or friends to help them. At least the problem of their accommodation is solved, for the beginning anyway."

Shabir startled and looked at his brother's face. Was Jamal implying anything at him? But no. There was no trace or hint of any underlying note in his words. Jamal was just presenting facts as they were. His face was honest and sincere as he continued, "I had to share a room with two other Asian boys, one from India, one from Bangladesh, who too had been lured by London's charm. To support myself, I had to take on low minor jobs, and I worked day and night, winter or summer. The house in which I rented and shared the room was damp and congested. The walls and ceilings were cracked and unpainted, and the wallpapers were peeling. The other rooms were as over-occupied as mine. It lacked proper heating and lighting facilities. The bathroom and kitchen were filthy. It was insecure and inadequate accommodation. I had to go many days without decent food. After three years of hard struggle, I was able to afford to rent a room for myself, in a Pakistani couple's house. They owned and lived in the house too. I had to share the kitchen and bathroom with them. Believe me, it was very inconvenient at times, but at least the house was clean, and the husband and wife were a nice pair. They became my *munh bole*" (verbal) "brother and sister-in-law. We all three needed someone to call our own in this land. So it was a mutual affection between us." Jamal Bhai paused a little, possibly remembering his verbal brother and sister-in-law.

"Then letters from Pakistan started coming from *Ama Ji* and *Aba Ji*" (Mother and Father). "In those days, phone calls were not common, so letters were the major source of communication. They wrote the same things over and over again, pleading me to come back. They were longing to see my face, and Ama Ji was yearning to tie, to see a *sehra* on my face" (to tie the floral chaplet around the groom's head). "She wanted to see me as bridegroom, married to a girl as beautiful as the moon and have a daughter-in-law as beautiful as the moon. I was upset. I didn't know what to do. I had toiled and laboured in this country for so long, endured hardship, and I didn't want to go back without gaining anything. I wanted to stay here permanently. I wanted British nationality. I went to Saleem Bhai and Razia Baji, (my verbal brother and sister-in-law, also my landlords), to ask for their opinion. They listened to what I had to say but politely refused to give me any advice or agree to be of any assistance in having my wish of staying here fulfilled. They didn't want to come between me and my family. They weren't going to be called family breakers. But yes, they would try to do something for me if they had my parents' permission." Jamal Bhai ran his fingers through his hair.

"I wrote a long letter to Ama Ji and Aba Ji, explaining everything, hiding nothing. Their reply arrived. Disappointed as they were, they had given me the permission to do whatever I felt was right for me. They wished me happiness. The letter was smudged here and there. Perhaps Ama Ji had written with tears in her eyes and some of the tears had fallen on the words spreading the ink. With sobbing heart, I touched the letter reverently with my eyes and kissed all the smudges with my lips. There were millions of parents like them giving up their sons for this country." Jamal Bhai's voice went a bit quiet before he continued.

"Sara's parents were Saleem Bhai and Razia Baji's acquaintances. So, through them, this marriage of convenience, as it is sometimes called, was arranged. But I was lucky. Sara was someone I fell in love with as soon as I saw her."

Jamal Bhai's face softened. A warm glow was in his eyes.

"Sara was a sales assistant when I married her. She continued to work after marriage. Saleem Bhai and Razia Baji treated her as their own daughter. Now that Sara was in the family way, I worked in the day and drove a taxi at night. We decided that we needed a house." Jamal Bhai was looking back on the early days of his marriage.

"Sara had some savings in the bank. So had I. It was enough for a deposit. After finding this reasonably priced house, we applied for a mortgage. The house is in our joint names. Sara has as much hand in purchasing this house as I have. She has worked equally hard to maintain this house. She continued to work till the birth of Bilal, our youngest son. After that, we agreed she should stop working. She needed a rest, and looking after the children was a full-time job anyway. She hasn't stopped working entirely though. She sews clothes, mostly shalwar kameezes for the neighbourhood, whenever she feels like it. I don't like her doing it, but it's her own choice."

Shabir remembered seeing the sewing machine and the bags of unsewn clothes in his brother and sister-in-law's bedroom.

"Yes," Jamal Bhai said softly, "I do feel I have been luckier than most. Sara is the best thing that has happened to me here."

He stood up, stretching, and wishing Shabir goodnight, he left the room, leaving Shabir to think his own thoughts.

Shabir couldn't understand Sara Bhabi's attitude. She was cool to him, avoided him as much as she could, and talked to him only when necessary. Sometimes Shabir would wonder about his sister-in-law's attitude but most of the time he would try to ignore her aloofness towards him.

He could still recall that, when she had once visited Pakistan, he had gone out of his way to please her. He had hired a car (even though he could hardly spare the money) just to take her around to visit relatives or friends, to go shopping or sightseeing. He had done his utmost to make her stay in Pakistan as comfortable and memorable as possible. She had been cheerful and talkative and had appreciated Shabir's intentions. Now it seemed she had erased that period from her memory. She shared no pleasant conversations with Shabir and hardly ever asked or enquired after her in-laws back in Pakistan.

Shabir just couldn't understand her attitude. He tried to comprehend her behaviour but couldn't, so he gave up.

Aside from that, Jamal Bhai was good to him, the children were fond of him, and he had no intention of doing or saying anything to upset this set-up. He was too grateful to his brother and his family here in England.

Some weeks after his arrival, Jamal Bhai said to Shabir, "I have found you a job. Now don't get too excited," he added as he saw the light leaping into Shabir's eyes. "It's nothing brilliant."

"I don't mind," said Shabir excitedly. "I'm here to do anything. I won't be ashamed of a small job. I have prepared myself for anything."

"Well, it's not that bad either." Jamal Bhai smiled at Shabir's enthusiasm. "You know that kebab shop in the high street."

Shabir nodded.

"The owner is an old acquaintance of mine. One of the boys working there is leaving soon. He's willing to take you on. He knows you are here on a visit visa and you haven't got a work permit. But you don't have to mention this to anyone."

"Okay," said Shabir. "When do I start?"

"From Monday. It's a part-time job. You'll work from four o'clock in the evening till midnight, or maybe later than that. Sometimes if needed, he might ask you to come before four. Does it suit you?"

"Yes. It does," said Shabir.

"Good. Well, that's settled. I will give you a duplicate key of the front door, so that you can let yourself in and out as you please. That way, no one will get disturbed."

So Shabir started his new job. The owner was pleasant by nature but a shrewd businessman at heart. Another boy, Ahmed, who was a student, worked alongside him.

Shabir enjoyed his work. It was a new experience for him. He met all types of people from different countries. He learned to use the till and to handle money, and his English got better. But it was also very dangerous, as he sometimes served difficult customers.

One night, a group of goras came to the shop and ordered takeaway naan and kebabs (thick chapatti cooked in a clay oven and grilled mincemeat on a skewer). They looked like thugs and had a menacing look about them. Shabir avoided looking at the pernicious men, and he went on preparing their food as they stood sullenly glowering at him. He had packed their order and was now at the till, telling them the amount they had to pay, when one of them, a pimply youth, picked up the bag, which Shabir had placed on the counter, and said glowering, "We've already paid you, mate." His breath smelt of drink.

"No you haven't," said Shabir, recoiling.

"Are you calling me a liar, you Paki?"

The others had gathered alongside their malicious pal and were staring at Shabir with hatred.

"Yes, because you haven't paid," Shabir said with a tone of despite.

One of the thugs, who had a long scar on one side of his cheek, leaned over and hit Shabir in the face. He held him tightly by the arms, his fingers digging painfully into Shabir's skin.

"Go for it," the scar-faced gora shouted as Shabir struggled to free himself.

The others obeyed his command. They picked up the chairs and smashed them on the floor. They toppled the tables, sending salt and pepper pots crashing on the ground. They kicked the counter and the cold drinks unit with their heavy boots.

Ahmed quickly dialled the number of the owner and then the police.

By the time the police arrived, the damage had been done. The hooligans had run away without paying, and Shabir, covering his bruised face with a scarf had hidden in one of the alleys behind the restaurant to avoid an encounter with the police. He didn't want to be caught out and get into any trouble as he was on a visit and was not allowed to work here. The police sympathetically listened to Ahmed and the owner, (who had managed to arrive just before they did, pretending he had been working there when all this had happened), noted down their statement, and left saying that they would keep a watch out in the future. After the police had left Shabir came back to the shop from his hiding place. The owner sent him home to tend to his bruises.

Another time, a young *kala* (black person) rushed into the shop and, quick as lightning, flashed a knife in Shabir's face. "Quick," he demanded. "Open the till."

Shabir was paralysed with fear. He stood there like a dummy, unable to move.

"Hurry up, man," the kala shouted. 'Are you deaf or somethin'? I said open the till—or I'll do you in."

"No." Shabir tried to collect his senses and put his hands on the till. "No. I won't open it."

Ahmed dashed up to him and pushed him away from the till.

"Do you want to die?" he screamed in Punjabi (language of Pakistan's Punjab region). "Don't be daft. Give him what he wants. He won't hesitate to stab you. For God's sake, let him have the money." Ahmed looked exasperated.

Shabir stared at him in surprise and fright.

The kala stood glaring at Shabir with the knife in his hand as Ahmed jabbed his fingers on the till. The kala thrust the knife in his pocket as the till opened and grabbed as much money as he could in his hands and ran out of the shop.

Shabir was still in a shocked state.

Ahmed, visibly shaken himself, explained, "In situations like these, think of your life first. Don't resist. Just give them what they want. Your life is more valuable."

"But that's cowardice, standing there, giving these thugs hard-earned money."

"Think of it this way. It's not your money. It's the owner's. And believe me, he has plenty. A few quids less won't make any difference to him. What would happen if you should die? Nothing. The kala would get away with murder, never to be caught. The owner would hire a new boy, and your family would cry for you for a while. Who would be the looser? You. Just remember, your life is more important. Why should you die so young for a few pounds? You are not a coward. You are just saving yourself. Bravery is stupidness in these matters."

Ahmed had made his point, and Shabir promised to be careful in future.

And that day, he was truly sad, when two Asian youths came in the shop. They were drug addicts. Their eyes were glazed and empty, their colour was sickly yellow, and their speech was sluggish. Shabir could hardly make out what they were saying. After ordering their food, they stumbled towards a table and slumped into the chairs.

Shabir wondered if he should throw some cold water over them or should give them a lecture on the harmful effects of drugs. *Who are the unfortunate parents?* He thought as he placed plates of food in front of the drugged boys.

They barely touched their food, talked vaguely, and smoked. At closing time, Shabir and Ahmed had to drag them out of the shop. They swore and flung out their arms as if to hit them; instead their arms flapped into the air and then fell to their sides, lifeless and weak. With much difficulty, Shabir and Ahmed managed to put them on the seats beside the bus stop and left them there.

But all was not doom and gloom. Shabir and Ahmed had fun with some customers—especially the regular ones. They came smiling and happy, laughed and joked loudly, talked in a good manner, and left Shabir and Ahmed in good moods.

For instance, a buoyant burly old English man always came in looking jolly and cheerful and told a joke with every sentence. Shabir marvelled at his sense of humour and his memory, which had stored so many jokes and quotes.

And other pleasant customers came too—like the girls of all different nationalities and colours. Some of them would be so stunning that Shabir couldn't help staring at them. But Amna's face was always in his eyes, hiding the other girls' faces.

Shabir was getting weary of the kebab shop. It had been fun at the beginning. He had enjoyed serving various types of customers. He had been amazed and amused when the goras ate kebabs with chutneys and "soo-sooed" when they felt the red chillies burning their throats. But now he found the work monotonous, and the sleepless nights were tiring him. He couldn't sleep properly in the day. He wanted a good night's sleep and wanted a daytime job. Jamal Bhai had promised to keep a lookout for him but had pressed that, in the meantime, Shabir should continue with his present work.

The money Shabir was earning was being kept in a building society account in Jamal Bhai's name. He had sent his parents some money several times, through a man who exchanged Pakistani rupees for pounds.

Shabir's parents' letter had arrived a few weeks later with lots of affection, gratitude, and blessings.

Jamal Bhai every now and then phoned Pakistan to enquire after their parents, so Shabir often got the chance to speak to them.

Shabir was trying to sleep in the daytime. He was feeling uncomfortable. Sara Bhabi was on the phone in the passage, and she hadn't bothered to lower her voice, as she had thought that he was sleeping.

"No, he's still here," she was saying to someone in the receiver.

"Yes. *Bahut ee museebat ae*" (Too much trouble). "No privacy at all. He comes in and out as if he owns the house."

"You've got to be kidding! Typical Pakistani man. Never lifts a finger to help around the house. I'm ashamed to invite guests because of the mess in the sitting room."

"Never washes the bathtub or mops the floor after he has a bath."

"Of course, it's all Jamal's fault. I told him a hundred times not to call him over. I—"

"No, I can't say that. Jamal wouldn't hear of it. You know how Pakistani men are. They'd do anything for their families. It's the women who have to make all the sacrifices. If it had been my brother, Jamal would have been screaming the place down."

"You're right. He shouldn't have been granted a visa in the first place. I was praying that the British Embassy would refuse him. They usually do with young men. His luck was with him."

"Oh, I don't know. I'm so fed up. You know, he's extended his visa for another six months. It seems we'll be lumped with him for the rest of our lives."

"The expenses are enough already. The mortgage. The bills. The food, etc., etc., but of course I can't make Jamal see that. *Toba, toba*" (Heaven forbid)."

Shabir's heart was cringing, shrivelling inside. He felt insulted and degraded. He fully understood the reason for Sara Bhabi's aloof and unfriendly attitude now. He had enjoyed their hospitality. He had utilized Jamal Bhai's house as his own—had, in fact, thought of it as his own his house. And Sara Bhabi's conversation with her friend, or whoever was on the other end of the conversation, had jolted him to the fact that this was not his own house.

Well, he had been a burden enough. He would have to do something about it. He would talk to Jamal Bhai, without seeming ungrateful, without mentioning Sara Bhabi's name, of course. He wasn't going to a home wrecker.

Shabir had left the kebab shop and was now working in a dry-cleaner's. He hated the work as soon as he started it. Cleaning and pressing clothes every day wasn't much fun. The room at the back was hot, stuffy, and suffocating, and the job was dull and depressing. He regretted leaving the kebab shop in such haste. At least there he'd met lots of people, and he'd had such good laughs with Ahmed and the customers. And he'd been able to look out of the shop at the crowd and at the traffic passing by.

His visa had been extended for another six months. He was now extremely worried about what would happen after the six months were over. But his main worry, for now, was to find an accommodation—a room maybe. How was he going to go on about his search without offending or hurting Jamal Bhai?

Many days passed, and he still couldn't gather enough courage to talk to Jamal.

One night, Jamal came, as usual, to have a chat with Shabir. Sharing a nightly conversation had become a habit for the two brothers ever since Shabir had joined the dry-cleaners.

Shabir sitting crossed legged on the sofa bed, searched for suitable words to explain his reasons for separate accommodation.

Jamal Bhai sitting on the sofa opposite Shabir, too, seemed preoccupied with some thoughts. After talking about this and that for a while, he leaned over and asked, "Look, Shabir, do you still want to stay in this country?"

"Of course I do, Jamal Bhai. What a question," he said.

"You know, after these six months are over, you'll have to go back, and because you have over stayed your visit, it's highly likely that you'll never be granted a British visa again."

"So, please, Jamal Bhai, what should I do?" Shabir asked worriedly.

"Okay." Jamal took a deep breath. "I have one solution for this problem. I have thought it over many times. It's the only solution I can find and . . . to me, it seems a reasonable one too. Listen Shabir." Jamal was clasping and unclasping his hands. He bowed his head and then lifted it and looked directly at Shabir's face. "You should get married to a girl from here with British nationality—like I did with Sara."

Shabir sprang up from the sofa bed and sat up straight, his face deathly pale.

Somewhere far away, Amna was crying.

"I . . . I can't . . . Amna . . . !" Shabir's voice broke.

Jamal Bhai raised the palm of his hand. "Yes, I know you love Amna—and always have. And I know you two have been promised to each other for as long as I can remember, perhaps from childhood. But, Shabir, this is your life's decision."

Amna's my life's decision too, Jamal Bhai. Without her all decisions are useless.

"You can't have life both ways," Jamal Bhai went on. "There are two roads open for you to choose from. The first road leads to Amna. Go back to Pakistan, marry her, and forget England. The second road leads to the completion of your long-time dream. Stay here, marry a British national, and forget Amna." He stopped and looked at Shabir's pale face. "I'm sorry, mere Bhai, but there's no middle course."

"Oh, but there is, Jamal Bhai, there is." Shabir seemed to be battling with himself. "Paper marriage."

Somewhere far away, Amna was laughing sarcastically in a crazed manner. *Stop it*, he wanted to shout. *I am not being unfaithful to you. I'm not. I'm not. It will only be a paper marriage. I won't touch her.*

He hated admitting it, but he'd had this thought for quite a while now. One of the boys from the dry-cleaners had planted this idea into Shabir's head. Nasir was involved with a gori. Shabir had seen the gori. She was fat and had blotchy skin and lanky hair filled with dandruff. Her teeth and fingertips were stained and yellow from chain-smoking. He had felt revolted by Nasir's choice and had told him so.

Nasir had laughed and said, "Who says I care for her. She's just a route to my British passport. As soon as I get it, I'm done with her."

"Paper marriages," said Jamal Bhai, "are out of date. They are no good these days. You never know who might tell on you. Rules and times have changed now. People have become wiser here. If someone's going to marry, even if it is to stay here, then why not for good? Stay with the spouse; have children and a real family life. It's beneficial for both sides. The girl and her parents are saved from the immigration trips and from the hindrances of the girl's in-laws. A lone son-in-law is more preferable, and the boy gets his wish to stay here. He has the full support of his wife and in-laws to set him up here—financially too, of course. In some cases like these, the in-laws might even give a deposit for a house as a part of the girl's dowry and the girl is the main bread earner. As I have told you before, it's a marriage of convenience, suitable and advantageous for both sides."

Jamal hesitated, took in Shabir's strained face, and then proceeded gravely. "I have known Mr and Mrs Waheed for some time now. They have five daughters and one son. They married their eldest daughter to a cousin in Pakistan. It was decided between both parties that the boy would be called over to England. It took them four years to do that. The time and money spent on these immigration *chakars*" (visits) "to Pakistan were immense. The girl didn't work, so she had to pay to have her 'work papers' made. She didn't own a house, so her brother transferred his house into her name. They had to do all that just to get their son-in-law over. And then, when he came, they helped to settle him here. Now they say they have learned their lesson. They don't want the same thing happening to their second daughter. If you wish and . . . give me your consent . . . I'll talk to them about your *rishta*" (match).

He waited for Shabir's response.

"I . . . I can't, Jamal Bhai. I can't hurt Amna." *And myself*, he added silently. *I'll die without her. She's my life blood.*

"Look, I respect Amna. She's a nice, lovely girl, and I'd hate to see her hurt. She's dear to me too. But you've got to understand. You can't always have life the way you want it. To gain something, you have to lose something. I know it's going to be hard, but . . ." Jamal spread out his hands helplessly. "It's your decision now."

"But, Amna . . ." Shabir's voice was weak.

Jamal stood up and looked at Shabir with compassion. His heart ached for his younger brother. Shabir looked so haggard, so downtrodden, as if life was trampling him, as if life was taking everything away from him.

"Why don't you sleep on it? You don't have to decide straight away. You've still got some time left," Jamal said gently, touching Shabir lovingly on the head. He went out of the room.

Shabir sat for a long time, staring at the palms of his hands. Circumstances were slipping from his hands. He was standing at a crossroads. He didn't know on which course life was going to take him.

Shabir was dreaming.

Amna is running in an endless desert. Her dupatta has slipped from her head onto her shoulder and is trailing behind her. It is sprinkled with sand. So is her hair and her face. Her shalwar kameez are rumpled, and they too are covered with sand.

The sun is scorching in the sky, and Amna's feet are blistered by the hot sand.

Amna is thirsty. Her throat and mouth are dry. Sand had settled on her parched lips. As she runs, she calls a word over and over again in a soundless voice. Shabir cannot comprehend or hear what she's saying. Maybe she's reciting a prayer.

Suddenly, Amna sees an oasis.

Shabir is leaning against a palm tree by the oasis. He is gazing straight ahead at something beyond Amna.

Amna flings her arms open wide and, still repeating that soundless word, she runs even faster towards the oasis.

As Amna approaches the oasis, it vanishes. What she had thought was an oasis was a mirage.

She screams out that soundless word and falls on her face in the hot sand.

Shabir woke up with a sudden start. The sweat was pouring from his face and body, and he was breathing heavily.

He knew now the word that Amna had been repeating soundlessly over and over again like a prayer.

It was his name.

Was Amna losing him?

Was she?

Was she?

No.

No.

Never.

Never.

Never.

The next morning while at breakfast, Shabir said to Jamal, "Jamal Bhai, I have to go back to Pakistan. I must. I cannot let Amna lose." He toyed with the food on his plate.

Jamal patted his hand. "I respect your decision. Of course you must go where your heart leads you." He picked up his fork.

"When do you want to go?"

"As soon as possible." Shabir broke a piece of bread vigorously.

"All right. The return air ticket I sent you should still be valid. Will you reserve your seat, or shall I do it for you?"

"No, it's all right. I'll do it myself." The piece of bread stuck in Shabir's throat.

"Okay, then. I'll see you in the evening." Jamal Bhai put his cup down. "Don't worry, yaar. Don't look so distressed."

After Jamal Bhai left for work, Shabir booked his seat with the airline office.

He told everyone at the dry-cleaner's he was leaving. He phoned Pakistan to inform his parents of his arrival.

He bought presents for his family and Amna and watched Sara Bhabi's good nature coming back. She chatted gaily with him and made silly, teasing jokes with him like a sister-in-law did with her younger brother-in-law. She even bought gifts for Amna and her in-laws. Shabir watched and listened to her with self-consciousness. He knew in his heart she was glad to be rid of him.

The children expressed their feelings individually. Usman said he would miss his uncle. Bilal was reluctant to leave Shabir's side once he had heard his chacha was going back. And Nazia had sat in his lap, put her arms around his neck, and asked, "Do you have to go back, Chacha?"

"Yes, beta, I do. I have to go back." He kissed her cheek.

"Will you come back?" she asked innocently.

Shabir sighed. "No, I don't think so . . ." He bit his lip. "At least . . . Oh, I don't know . . ."

Tonight was his last night in this house. He had packed his belongings and had put them neatly in the corner of the sitting room. He was truly ready to go.

Sara Bhabi had cooked a delicious meal for him, and Jamal Bhai, as usual, had a chat with him before going upstairs.

Shabir was having difficulty sleeping. Images and voices jumbled in his mind and ears. He tossed and turned, trying to block them out. He would go insane if they didn't stop. He put his hands to his head.

Amna was accusing, "It's your dream, Shabir. Not mine."

His mother was saying, "Well, you must go if that's your wish."

The man at the embassy stressed, "That country is like an octopus. It will wrap you with its tentacles. You won't be able to free yourself."

Amna was crying, "I'll wait, but will you come back?"

Shabir was saying, "I have to go to Amna, Jamal Bhai. I have to."

The man at the embassy sneered, "Liar. Hypocrite."

The old baba was weeping in the embassy, "Oh, my son . . . oh, my grandchildren."

Jamal Bhai was consoling, "You are lucky you have someone to support you. When I came, I was alone."

The man at the embassy was saying savagely, "They can stuff their England."

Amna was running, running in a desert. She was calling out to him.

The gora thug in the kebab shop was leering in Shabir's face, "You Paki. Go back to Pakistan."

The fashionable woman at the embassy was fanning herself delicately with a piece of paper. "What is here in Pakistan? Nothing but heat, dirt . . ."

Amna was pleading, "I'll eat plain roti, drink plain water. Just stay with me here."

Jamal Bhai was being philosophical, "To gain something, you have to lose something."

Shabir was running an ink pen over the lines of kismet on the palms of his hands. The ink was spreading . . . spreading . . .

Ahmed was shouting, "Your life's too precious."

His father was shaking his head sadly and saying, "This hookah doesn't work properly. I'll have to buy a new one."

His mother was hugging him. She smelt of onions and ghee.

Amna was sniffing. "No, I'm not crying. It's just the smoke."

The man at the embassy was sneering, "Liar. Hypocrite."

The students at the embassy were chatting and laughing and throwing their hand, palm down over the other's hand, palm up.

Aslam was begging, "Please, Shabir Bhai, please call me over to England."

The "visa rejected" young man of Shabir's age was walking out of the embassy with his head hung to the ground.

Shabir's friends were saying enviously, "You lucky devil. Just imagine going to England."

Sara Bhabi was complaining, "We are lumped with him."

Nasir was laughing, "She's my route to British passport."

His gori girlfriend was bringing her blotchy face closer to Shabir. She smelt of cigarettes.

Amna was making senseless lines on the bricked floor by the clay stove.

Jamal Bhai was insisting, "The only way to stay here is to marry a British national."

Amna was hurting. "You give me wounds . . ."

Ahmed was explaining. "Think of your life first."

The man at the embassy was snide. "Ah, I see you don't like reality."

Shabir sprung up from the sofa bed. He was going to wring the man at the embassy's neck. He put out his hands as if to grab him. An empty void filled his hands.

Shabir's head felt heavy. His heart was sinking. He didn't know why. He should be happy. He was going back. To his mother and father. To Amna. So why were his heartbeats so dull?

Jamal Bhai was driving him to the airport. The children had hugged him over and over again before going to school. Sara Bhabi had given him her best wishes and had decided to say her goodbye from home.

The car sped on. Both Jamal and Shabir were unusually quiet. Shabir felt weak and exhausted from conflicting within himself. He rested his head on the back of the seat.

Earlier this morning, Jamal Bhai had said, with tears in his eyes, "I know I was totally against your coming to England at first, but I want you to know, it's been a pleasure having you. You don't know how much I've appreciated your company. I have lived in this country for so long without any blood relations. I had forgotten how it feels to have someone who's my own near me. Someone to pour my heart out to. Someone to share my problems with. To share my happiness and my sorrow with. You have made me realise the values of family ties and bonds. Thank you for coming. May Allah bless you."

Shabir hadn't known what to say. His emotions were in a chaos. He wanted to see his family. But was he glad? He wanted to go back—but not like this, empty-handed. He hadn't gained anything. He hadn't achieved anything. What exactly he wanted to gain or achieve, he didn't know. But he hadn't meant to go back to Pakistan like this.

He turned his head from side to side. He just couldn't—he just wouldn't—watch his dream, his expectations shattering . . . crumbling . . . crushed. He put his hands to his burning eyes and shouted, "Stop, Jamal Bhai. Stop. Turn the car back. I can't go . . . . I don't want to . . . like this. Turn the car around. Please turn the car back."

Sara Bhabi was going to cry to see him back again.

Shabir's marriage to Hina was arranged.

He sat quietly and watched everything and everyone with empty eyes. He felt bewildered, unhappy, and depressed. What was life doing to him?

Shabir's prospective in-laws, Jamal Bhai, and Sara Bhabi embraced, kissed, and congratulated each other. They were all gathered in Jamal Bhai's sitting room. The sweetmeats were brought, and everyone sweetened his or her mouth. Someone pushed a *laddoo* (a type of sweetmeat) between Shabir's lips. It tasted poisonous. He niggled it down.

The marriage date was set for next month. Shabir had lost Amna and had gained Hina. He had attained his dream to stay here. He didn't know whether to laugh or cry.

Mrs Waheed, Hina's mother, stroked Shabir's head customarily and asked lovingly, "Beta, would you prefer dowry or money?"

Shabir looked helplessly at Jamal, who came to his rescue at once.

"No, *behnji*" (good sister). "Neither money, nor dowry. You have already given us your most valuable thing—Hina. That's all we want."

After the merry guests had left, Jamal phoned Pakistan to inform the family of Shabir's forthcoming wedding. Shabir didn't want to speak to his mother or anyone. He didn't have the courage or the strength. He wanted to crawl away, to hide somewhere, but Jamal Bhai was beckoning him over. He had to listen to the phone. It was his mother.

"Shabir, beta," she wailed on the other end. "What have you done? What shall I tell Amna or her parents? How shall I tell them? This news will kill them. You have brought dishonour to us. How will we cope with this disgrace . . . the humiliation?"

The receiver fell from Shabir's hand. He was shaking violently. Jamal Bhai sensed Shabir's state of mind and hurriedly put an arm around him. He picked up the receiver and said quickly, "Ama Ji, I'll ring you again . . . . Maybe tomorrow. *Khuda Hafiz*" (goodbye).

He led the shaking and shivering Shabir to the sofa and, holding him close, calmed him, soothed him, and comforted him till the shaking had subsided.

Shabir and Hina were married with all the usual gaiety, cheerfulness, and joyfulness that were an essential part of an Asian wedding.

Jamal Bhai played the part of a proud older brother with dignity. The three children were having fun in their own way. Even Jamal Bhai's old landlords, Saleem Bhai and Razia Baji, were invited to celebrate the wedding. Ahmed and Nasir and the jolly old English man too had come to enjoy the event.

Sara Bhabi was hostile towards Shabir. She had put on a brave face for the wedding, but Shabir knew she was seething inside. He saw contempt in her eyes for him. He couldn't reproach her. She had the right to feel this way. Jamal Bhai had taken the weight of all the costs of this wedding on his shoulders. Shabir was indeed indebted to both of them.

In spite of all this, there was much fun, noise, and laughter; much playing of the *dholki'* (percussion instrument, a small drum), singing, and dancing; much colourful clothes, perfumes, and jewellery; and plenty of food and drinks.

Jamal Bhai had hired a video cameraman to film all the events of the wedding, including the *mehndi* or r*asm e henna* or' *tael'*(henna ceremony or oil ceremony, held the night before the wedding day, traditionally held separately for the bride and groom when henna is placed on couple's hand and oil is rubbed into couple's hair by the near to kin guests), the baraat (the actual wedding day, bridegroom's wedding procession to be received by the bride's family on the wedding day and official wedding ceremony to be), the *walima* (reception, held day after the wedding when the groom's family invites the bride's family and guests to publicize the marriage).

Yes, weddings were for all to enjoy themselves, and everyone participated delightfully in these joyous occasions.

Apart from Jamal Bhai, no one noticed Shabir's anguish. Shabir had watched the wedding preparations lifelessly. He felt as if he was living outside himself these days. It was not him but another Shabir going through all this.

His rasm e henna had been celebrated at Jamal Bhai's house last night, while Hina's had been celebrated at her parents' house.

The baraat was received by Hina's family in a marriage hall. Relatives, friends, guests, and neighbours had all gathered to celebrate this happy occasion.

Shabir sat on the sofa, placed on the stage, which was specially decorated for the bride and bridegroom. His face looked deathly white. It seemed as if all the blood had been wrung out from his body.

Hina, dressed in her bridal attire, surrounded by her sisters and her friends, was walking towards him, down the aisle. He wanted to run away. No, he wanted to stay. He had to stay. He grasped the edge of the sofa tightly.

She was dressed in a bright red glittering wedding *lehnga* (the long skirt and short blouse typical of an Asian wedding) and adorned with gold jewellery ornaments. The centre of her long, wide red, resplendent dopatta to match the lehnga was secured firmly on her head with hair pins, while one corner was pinned on her one shoulder and the other corner fell at her back. Her hands and feet were decorated with henna. Her bridal make-up had been applied by an expert beautician. Her sisters and friends sat her down next to Shabir.

The camera and video lights were flashing. The video was to be sent to Pakistan—a knife in the heart of Shabir's loved ones.

The *nikah* (official Islamic matrimonial service) was read out by a *maulvi* (Muslim priest), and both Shabir and Hina accepted and signed the *nikah nama* (matrimonial documents) witnessed by the whole marriage group. After the nikah ceremony was performed there was a loud a cheer of '*mubarak* ho' (congratulations) and much embracing between the bride and bridegroom's sides, women embracing women, men embracing men.

A crowd of well-wishers, from both of the bride and groom's sides, had gathered around bride and groom.

One of Hina's sisters surmised, "The *lara*" (bridegroom) "seems shy."

"He won't be tonight," someone shouted from above the noise.

A roar of laughter sounded from the crowd.

Someone observed, "The bridegroom looks weak."

"Hina will make him drink milk daily. He'll get his energy back," someone else assured loudly.

Another roar of laughter followed.

Someone perceived, "The bridegroom looks as though he doesn't speak much."

"He knows his place already. From now on our Hina will speak, and he will listen," someone else announced shrilly.

"The bridegroom appears rather serious," someone noted, regarding Shabir.

"He'll be laughing tomorrow. Just wait and see after tonight," someone bellowed out at full volume.

Laughter, rejoicing, jokes, and jests—was there no end to this day?

"The bridegroom looks tired," someone noticed with pity.

There's still the night left," someone else revelled in a booming voice.

This time the shriek of laughter was ear-splitting.

Soon it was time for *rukhsati* (the departure or sending off the bride, when the bride leaves her parent's house with the groom and her in-laws to start her married life).

With the Quran held over their heads by a guest member, for blessing, Shabir and Hina walked from the stage to the exit of the hall, where outside on the road a decorated car awaited to take them to Jamal Bhai's house.

Jamal Bhai had decorated his bedroom as the bridal chamber. Shabir couldn't look Sara Bhabi in the eyes. He knew a silent row had been going on for days between the husband and wife over this matter. Shabir felt ashamed and hung his head whenever he saw his sister-in-law. He knew she was looking daggers at him. He didn't blame her. She had to sacrifice her bedroom. And it was a big sacrifice. He understood that.

How many people must he hurt to gain access to British nationality?

He'd tried to talk Jamal Bhai out of offering his bedroom but Jamal Bhai would hear none of it.

"Nonsense. You can't spend your wedding night on a sofa bed."

He had weakly suggested a hotel, but Jamal Bhai dismissed the idea. "You have a house. Why stay in a hotel?"

And lovingly, he pushed Shabir up the stairs, where Hina, his bride, was waiting for him.

The stairs heaved with each step he climbed.

Deceiver!

He stood in front of the bedroom door with his hand on the doorknob.

His heart wept.

Forgive me, Amna. Forgive me.

He opened the door. The door creaked.

Betrayer!

He went in and closed the door.

Hina sat, a bundle of red, on the bed, with her head bowed.

He sat in front of her. The bed squeaked.

Promise breaker!

With trembling hands, he lifted the red glittering dupatta that covered her head and face.

His heart leapt.

Amna? No. Hina.

Forgive me Amna, forgive me, for giving your rights to someone else.

Hina was looking at him expectantly. He knew what was expected of him. He looked at her henna-coloured hands. The nails were painted bright red, and the fingers were decorated with gold rings.

He took her hand in his. The bangles jingled.

Heartbreaker!

He pulled a ring out of his pocket and slipped it on her finger as a part of her *munh dekhai* (showing of the bride's face to her bridegroom for the first time after nikah).

He closed his eyes. He drew Hina close to him.

Unfaithful!

He had saved his dream.

Somewhere far away, Amna was sobbing heart wrenchingly in the dark.

Shabir had taken two weeks off from work for the wedding. Jamal Bhai had forced Shabir and Hina to take a short honeymoon. They went sightseeing around London. All the buildings and places that had once seemed unreachable and alluring to Shabir held no charm now. It was a part of human nature. As long as something was out of your reach, it was valuable. Once you attained it, it lost its value.

Hina, Shabir found out, was a most unselfish girl. She never complained or grumbled. And if at times she sensed Shabir's withdrawal, she didn't mention it. She adored Shabir with a simplicity and honesty that was touching in itself. She was also a most compromising girl. She respected Jamal Bhai and Sara Bhabi and got on well with them and the children.

She had left school with no ambitions of higher studies or a career. She was, at heart, a truly homely girl. Sometimes she reminded Shabir so much of Amna that it hurt him.

She mostly spoke English, but she also spoke broken Punjabi, which sounded charming to the ear. Though she had been born and bred in London, she was a typical Asian girl at heart. She wore English clothes, but she also loved wearing shalwar kameezes and heavy sparkling jewellery. She liked wearing arm full of bangles and anklets around her ankles.

Shabir had found it impossible to believe that she had never been to Pakistan.

"I don't believe it." He shook his head in amazement.

"Well, Mum did say she took me once, when I was a baby," she answered innocently.

"Didn't you ever want to go?" he asked, still amazed.

"Of course I did. And I do now. With you." She looked appealingly at him.

Shabir caught his breath. At that moment she had looked at him exactly as Amna used to when she was in a tender mood. A wave of pain swept over his heart. He turned away. Women were the same all over the world. *Don't*, he begged silently. *Don't trust me too much. I'm not worth it.*

Now the time had come when Shabir really had to do something about finding him and his wife a separate accommodation.

He had forced Jamal Bhai and Sara Bhabi to return to their own bedroom, after using it for the first couple of nights. His heart was full of gratitude, and he couldn't take any more advantage of their generosity.

Sara Bhabi's attitude towards Hina was gentle, but it remained the same with him. He could hear her banging pots and pans irritably in the kitchen when he was around. It wasn't her fault, he told himself. She needed her independence and privacy.

He was afraid of an open disgruntlement in the house. He would have to do something before it happened.

He couldn't risk losing his brother or bhabi. A move on was imperative.

So that night, he respectfully made his request to Jamal. "Jamal Bhai," he began, "please don't be offended or think or that I am being ungrateful, but with your permission, Hina and I would like to apply for a council accommodation."

Jamal regarded Shabir sadly and then nodded his head in agreement. "Yes, Shabir. I think the time for that has come now." Then he said in a low voice, "I know Sara hasn't—"

Shabir quickly reached out and put a hand on Jamal's mouth. "Don't, Jamal Bhai, don't say anything. Sara Bhabi has been wonderful to me. She let me stay in her home and didn't let me wander about in the streets. I value her very much. For me, she's a mother, sister, and a bhabi all rolled into one. You don't know how much I appreciate and respect her. I have no complaints whatsoever against her. I shall always be grateful for what she has done for me. Letting anyone stay in your home for such a long time is not easy, I know. Has anyone ever seen a bhabi as big-hearted as her?" he asked tremulously.

Sara, who had been on the point of entering the sitting room, overheard Shabir. Her heart automatically cleared towards him. Quietly, she backed away from the door.

Jamal Bhai's smile was a little shaky. "Well, this house was rather crowded, wasn't it?"

Shabir smiled back. His lips were quivering, "Yes it was rather. And I can't sleep with my wife on the sofa bed for the rest of my life, now can I?"

Both of the brothers laughed tremulously and then hugged each other tearfully.

Shabir and Hina moved into a two-bedroom council flat. The flat was on the fifth floor. There was a lift (which hardly ever worked properly) as well as the stairs. It was a dark and dreary building, but the flat itself was spacious. It needed tidying up; otherwise, it was reasonable enough to live in.

It was near the main road and a walkable distance from the bus stop. So it was easy for Shabir and Hina to travel and get to wherever they wanted to go.

Jamal Bhai as usual had helped him in furnishing the flat in every way he could. Sara Bhabi was pleasant to him now, and she and Hina got on very well. It surprised Shabir that no "famous rivalry" existed between the two sisters-in-law.

Both husband and wife and the children would pop in almost every night to give them company and to make their hearts settle in the new place, so that they didn't feel too alone. If some day for some reason they couldn't come, they would phone and enquire how the newly weds were getting along. On some days, Shabir and Hina would go over to Jamal Bhai's and Sara Bhabi's to have dinner and come back to the flat at night.

Sometime after moving into the flat, a letter arrived from Shabir's mother. Shabir opened it with trembling hands.

His mother had written:

Aslaam O Alaikum.

Payare beté, sukhi raho (Dear son, live well).

Beté, I am a mother, so it's easy for me to forgive you for what you have done. I can cover up and lie for you. But tell me, what was Amna's fault?

When she heard of your marriage to Hina, she took an overdose of sleeping pills. She was found out in time and was rushed to the hospital. With proper treatment and care, she survived. Though she's discharged from the hospital now, she's like a living corpse. Every day she sits on her peerhi in her yard and, with empty eyes gazes at the front door of her house. Poor Amna!

I tried to undo a little bit of what you had done. I went to her parents, folded my hands in front of them, begged for forgiveness, and asked for Amna's rishta for your younger brother, Aslam. I thought I was being wise and fair, but Amna, on hearing this, screamed and screamed till she fainted. Her mother joined her hands in front of me and said bitterly, "What your one son has done to us is enough to last us for the rest of our lives. Don't keep ripping our sores. Now leave us to face our misery." And with that, both husband and wife cried so heartrendingly that I came back from their house even more aggrieved. I wish no parents have to go through this kind of pitiable state. I feel and understand their affliction.

But, beta, as I said before, I can forgive you, for I have a mother's heart. So I wish you and Hina happiness. May you prosper each day. Allah bless you.

Your mother,

Zainab Bibi

Shabir squeezed the letter in his hand. He clenched his jaws so hard that they hurt. His eyes were burning, and the lump in his throat was suffocating him. He couldn't breathe. He had to get out. He walked blindly out of the flat. The lift was out of order as usual. He kicked on the door viciously and walked down the dark stairs. The smell of urine in the staircase was as sharp as ever. Usually, Shabir spat on the floor and cursed whoever had messed the the stairs, but today, he was past caring.

The pain in his heart was getting worse. He walked on unheeding, unseeing, and uncaring. He walked past Mr Patel's corner shop, past the primary school, past the gurdwara, past the petrol station, past the mandir, through the high street, past the hospital, past the church, past the nursery, past the mosque, past the main traffic lights, and entered a park.

"Poor Amna!" His mother had written. She sits on her peerhi in the yard of her house and gazes at the front door.

He walked fast.

His mother had asked for Amna's rishta for Aslam.

He walked faster . . . faster.

Poor Amna!

He started running. Amna had tried to commit suicide because of him.

He wanted to hurt himself, to inflict some sort of pain on himself.

He wanted to bang his head on that tree till it bled.

Poor Amna!

He was panting now. The tree was getting nearer, and . . . He stopped suddenly—inches away from the tree—and laughed.

Poor Amna!

She had always been emotional. She always took everything so seriously. She had tried to commit suicide for him. And he wasn't even worth it.

It was funny. It was hilarious. It was hysterical. He laughed and laughed and laughed, till completely spent and drained of all strength, he fell on his knees in front of the tree, sobbing wildly.

An Englishman walking his dog in the park gave Shabir a spiteful look. *These foreigners*, he thought haughtily with flared nostrils, *they are a bunch of weirdoes. Look at that one over there, bent on his knees. Crying and laughing together. Probably a religious fanatic, worshipping a tree.*

You never knew what they'd do next. Better to keep away from them.

He whistled to his dog and called, "Lovey, Lovey, come on, darling. Let's go."

As he walked away, the Englishman turned his head, out of curiosity, to have a last look.

The foreigner was lying on the grass, doubled up as if in great pain.

It was nearly dark when Shabir came to himself, the letter still clutched in his hand. His head was throbbing, and he felt sick from the mental torture he had been through. He didn't know how long he had lain there, but he did know that today he had buried Amna's memories, alive, in a remote corner of his heart, never to be uncovered again.

They had been screaming and crying as he had thrown the soil of his betrayal on them. They hadn't wanted to be buried. They had battled with him to stay alive, nearly killing him.

To gain something, you have to lose something, Jamal Bhai had said.

He had lost Amna forever. No, not lost—had given up Amna . . . a long time ago. And with a shock, he realised that he had given her up when he had decided to come to England.

The pain-filled screams of Amna's memories were still echoing in his ears as he walked unsteadily out of the park.

The letter was squeezed tightly in his fist. He tried to throw the letter in a bin, but his fist wouldn't open. He tried to unlock his fingers from the letter with his other hand but couldn't free it. He bent his head and bit his hand hard. He screamed out in pain as his fist snapped open and the letter fell in the bin.

Amna's fears had been just. This country had won.

Shabir had left the dry-cleaners. Now that he was permitted to stay and work in this country, he hoped and searched for better employment. He was experienced in office work in Pakistan, and he anticipated, optimistically, that this ability would be an advantage to him. He took up computer classes to better his job prospects.

He scanned the newspapers daily and applied for the vacancies he felt were suitable for him. He would attend every interview he was called for and then be politely refused because, he would be told, his Pakistani qualifications, experiences, and English were not of a standard to fill the requirement of the particular job.

Shabir felt frustrated. Sometimes he felt that maybe he was discriminated against because he was an Asian.

As time passed, the will to find a better employment left him. He'd had such high expectations when he'd come to England. Now he was getting disillusioned. It was hard to accept that London had so little to offer him.

It was difficult for a healthy and energetic young man like him to stay idle for long. He took a job at the local grocery shop as a cashier and started taking driving lessons.

Jamal Bhai and family had come to see baby Omer. Ever since Hina had returned from the hospital, a week ago, with baby Omer in her arms, the family had been coming daily.

The children were delighted with Omer and gathered around him, squabbling with each other to be the first to hold him.

"My children, they don't let me have any peace in the evening. As soon as I come in from work, they start pestering me. 'Dad we want to see Omer. Let's go to see him.' There's nothing for me to do but bring them," Jamal Bhai told Shabir laughingly. And then had added, "To be quite honest, my heart gets restless to see Omer too."

Sara Bhabi was sitting with Hina. She was giving her tips and was telling her about her practised remedies on children. "If he cries at night, just warm a bit of ghee and then rub it on his chest and stomach. It soothes the child. I didn't use to believe in all this. I thought they were all old women's tales. My mother told me to try it on Usman . . ." she was saying.

Shabir sat with Jamal.

"What happened about Bilal's school, Jamal Bhai?" Shabir asked.

Jamal sighed. "Nothing, so far. I"m not sending him to school till something's done about it."

Shabir looked at Bilal. He had started secondary school this year. Previously the boy had enjoyed school and was awilling and apt student. He'd been good at his studies and polite to the teacherswho were pleased with his behaviour and progress.

Recently, he had started sulking and throwing tantrums in the morning, unwilling to go to school.

Sara Bhabi had ignored his behaviour at first, thinking it was just a phase he was going through. But as the phase grew longer, she started worrying. The boy was frightened to go to school and had lost his appetite. She tried talking, but Bilal shut his mouth tightly and stared her white-faced and wide-eyed.

She continued coaxing and persuading. Finally, he had broken down and admitted that he was being bullied by some older boys at school. He was picked on and pushed around, and any article or food he brought in his packed lunch from home was taken away from him by force. He was threatened that he'd be beaten if he told anyone what was going on.

He dreaded going to school because the boys were planning to "rush" him. He had fearfully told a teacher whom he trusted. The teacher had looked at him unbelievingly and betrayed his trust.

Sara Bhabi was aghast. She and Jamal Bhai at once went to the school to make a complaint to the headmistress, who had seemed very attentive and sympathetic. She had assured them that she would look into the matter urgently.

Jamal Bhai had demanded that this matter should be dealt with very seriously, and firm action should be taken against the bullies.

The headmistress had replied formally that it was important for her to understand the nature of these incidents, and she would be unable to take any sort of action till she had talked to the boys Bilal had pointed out. "But," she'd continued, "it's very important to inform. If Bilal had informed of these unpleasant incidents earlier, this matter would have been dealt with by now without reaching this stage."

"We told you already he was scared. The bullies threatened him. But when they planned to 'rush' him, he told a teacher, who didn't pay any attention to him," said Sara Bhabi, looking visibly more upset.

The headmistress replied, "I'll talk to that teacher too, as to why he didn't heed Bilal's request." She stopped for a while and looked at them and then went on, "As a parent, you have strong feelings of revenge and anger. It's understandable. It's very painful to feel helpless when a child we love is hurting. We feel concerned and upset too when this happens. Believe me, this matter will be dealt with swiftly and effectively."

She looked at her watch. Jamal Bhai and Sara Bhabi got up to leave.

"I'll inform you what steps will be taken when I have talked to the boys involved," she said as she let them out.

A couple of days later, the headmistress called Jamal Bhai and Sara Bhabi to her office. "I have talked to the boys that Bilal named, and they have all denied any involvement in this matter." She paused, waiting for a reaction. She considered their silent faces for a bit, and then carefully choosing her words, she said, "Children have tendencies to make things up—to exaggerate. Sometimes a child may invent all these incidents to attract attention—perhaps of parents, if they feel ignored or—"

"Are you implying that Bilal is lying?" Jamal Bhai broke in heatedly. "Or is it that you really don't want to be aware of what's happening in your school? You want to cover up this incident, don't you, for the fear of your school's reputation?" Jamal Bhai was livid. He stared at the headmistress fixedly.

The headmistress looked at him with distaste and said coldly, "I'm not implying anything, Mr Jamal. It's a fact. Sometimes it happens. And I am very well aware this problem exists, not only in our school, but in other schools all over the country. Our school has a clear behaviour management policy. We—"

"So you are not going to do anything, are you? Well, we'll see."

Jamal Bhai stormed out of the office, vowing to take the matter further.

"And have you?" inquired Shabir.

"Yes I did. I complained to the local education authority, but they seem to side with the headmistress, reluctant to take it any further, hoping that, given time, the matter would get cold and fade out."

"And has it?" asked Shabir doubtfully.

"I don't know." Jamal Bhai spread out his hands, exasperated. "We'll have to see. They are all prejudiced and racists at heart. The big talk of eradicating racism and bullying at all levels of society is nothing but a load of wind. Where are equal rights and justice? We have contributed so much to this country. We have given the best years of our lives to it. Surely we deserve better than we are getting."

A few days later, Jamal told Shabir that he had changed Bilal's school; the new school was some distance away, so Sara would drive Bilal to and from.

Shabir wondered. What if the same thing happened in Bilal's new school? Would Jamal Bhai or parents like him keep changing their children's school?

Jamal Bhai had been right when he had said that London was not all bright lights and glamour.

As time went by, Shabir saw the other side of London, which he had never thought possible when he'd been in Pakistan. This other side had opened his eyes and shown him scenes of misery, poverty, and distress.

He saw homeless people sleeping in streets, benches, doorways, or wherever they could find shelter, even in cardboard boxes. He saw street children and squatters. He saw beggars (he had thought beggars only existed in poor countries like Pakistan) in high streets and tube stations, playing musical instruments for money and sitting in subways with placards stating, "homeless and hungry" by their sides. He saw tramps searching the dustbins by the roadsides for morsels of food and cans and bottles of leftover drinks. He saw unemployed people, anxious and depressed with low self-esteem.

And it seemed that everyone was on the dole in this country, claiming some sort of benefits with sincerity or pretexts.

In spite of all this, the charm of London was the same as ever. Immigrants kept arriving at an alarming rate with hopes of better standards of living. They were everywhere, and there was no stopping them. Somehow or another, they managed to reach England.

Nostalgia for Pakistan was creeping over Shabir now. But he couldn't afford to be consumed by it. The time wasn't right yet.

Jamal Bhai was planning to set up a grocery shop. He often came over to Shabir's to discuss the possibility of the two brothers working in one shop.

Shabir agreed to the idea readily. He was fed up with working unsuitable hours and low-paying jobs. He needed something permanent and secure. He showed his enthusiasm by going around in search of a shop. Several important points had to be considered before making a final decision. The location was the most important one.

Jamal Bhai's children were growing up. He himself was a father of two now. He contemplated the possibilities of dispute erupting between the children of the two brothers over the shop. He had to bear it in mind that this might create a big problem in the future. But that was still a way to go yet. He would cross that bridge when he'd come to it.

Eventually, the brothers found a shop that went straight to their hearts. It was a shop in the middle of a neighbourhood. No other shops were around, and the chances of it working were good.

After Jamal and Shabir had gone through the necessary procedures, the shop opened. Both of the brothers worked hard, patiently, and determinedly.

The shop improved day by day, and it started pulling in customers.

Usman, Jamal Bhai's eldest son had turned into an adolescent. He wore designer jeans and leather jackets and walked with a swagger. He had an ear pierced and adorned it with a stud or a small earring. He was always having his hair cut in various shapes and designs, covered with gel.

Shabir would watch him amusedly. On some days, he would be loud and aggressive; on other days, he would be cool and aloof with a mind-your-own-business look about him. And sometimes he would be a typical Asian, wearing shalwar kameez, going to the mosque, asking his mother to cook him samosas (pastry filled with various spicy fillings) or kebabs, and the like.

Shabir would try to figure who the boy was trying to imitate—the kalas, the goras, or the typical British Asian youth of his generation—and then decide that he was mixture of all three and leave it at that.

He was, in all, a nice, pleasant and handsome boy. Shabir genuinely loved him. He would come to the shop whenever he was in the mood to help out, but as Jamal Bhai didn't encourage him much because of his education, his attention was less inclined towards the shop.

Usman continuously listened to English music. He would have his walkman in his pocket and headphones on his ears and would sing and shake and shiver with the music.

"Hi, Chacha," he said as he came into the shop. "I've just bought a new CD. You should really listen to it. It's bad. Bad band. Bad lyrics. Bad music." He praised his choice of music so much that Shabir felt compelled to listen to it.

Usman, pleased that at last his chacha had shown some interest in his choice of English music, happily put the walkman in Shabir's hand and the headphones over his chacha's ears and turned the volume full. A mixture of howling, screaming, screeching, scratching, grating, and God knows what bellowed into Shabir's ears. He couldn't make heads or tails of the music or the words.

Usman was looking at him with anticipation.

Shabir smiled at him and endured the cacophony for a while. In the end, he gave up and handed the walkman and headphones back to Usman.

"Bad, in'it?" Usman asked hopefully.

"Yeah. Wicked," replied Shabir (he was beginning to use these words now) with a finger moving fiercely in his earhole. The music had nearly blocked his ears.

In future, he vowed to himself, he would stick to his own safe Pakistani and Indian music.

Shabir disliked the flat life thoroughly. He had gone through his share of the usual problems that the other flat dwellers sometimes experienced.

Once, his flat had been burgled. The burglar(s) had broken in through the kitchen window. It was fortunate that, on that day, Hina and the children were visiting her parents and he had been at the shop, so he and his family had escaped physical harm. He had reported the incident to the police. The police had come, walked around the flat, looked at the ripped and thrown stuff on the floor, asked some questions, noted a few things down, and left, saying that they would do everything to catch the burglar(s) and that, in the meantime, it would be a good idea if they had the kitchen window mended to avoid any more future burglaries.

Twice Shabir had been mugged on the flat's stairs. Once, he hadn't had much cash on him, but the thugs had taken whatever he'd had and had left him unharmed. The other time, they had tried to snatch his watch and wallet and had kicked and punched him when he'd tried to resist.

But last night had been the worst experience. He, Hina, and the children were returning home after visiting his in-laws. They had gotten off at the bus stop on the main road and were walking towards their block of flats when they had encountered a gang of white hooligans in the compound. The yobs were drinking and laughing and kicking cans and bottles on the ground.

"Look, a Paki family," one of them had jeered, hurling an empty can of beer at Shabir and his family as they cut across and followed a pathway to reach their block.

Shabir and Hina had ignored the louts and tried to walk past.

A pockmarked, pimply youth had stepped in front of Shabir and hit him with his shoulder.

"You wanna fight, Paki." He made a fist with his hands and punched Shabir in the stomach "Come on; fight me," he urged. "I'm gonna lick you." He stood in front of Shabir, glaring insolently at him.

Shabir was burning inside. His hands curled, and his nostrils flared. He flung out his arm furiously to retaliate.

At once, Hina put her hand on his arm and restrained him. "Don't Shabir," she pleaded in Panjabi. "There are too many of them. The children might get hurt."

Why was it that every time he wanted to strike back at unfairness, someone stopped him for one reason or another? It had been Ahmed once, in the kebab shop, when the kala thug had tried to rob them. Now it was Hina. He looked at her. A frightened look on her face read, *for the children's sake, Shabir, for the children.*

The pimply youth was smiling maliciously at Shabir. The rest of the gang stood, watching malevolently. One movement from Shabir, and they would pounce on him.

"Quick," said Hina, "pick Omer up."

Still looking at the malicious youth in front of him, Shabir slowly bent down and picked Omer up, and hugging him close to his heart, he, along with Hina, made a dash towards the stairs.

The gang bowled over with baleful laughter. Shabir could hear them hooting and using foul language.

On reaching the stairs, Hina quickly snatched Zainab (named after Shabir's mother) from her pushchair, and leaving it where it was, she ran up the stairs

Shabir, with Omer in his arms, looked around to see if the thugs were following.

The yobs stood there jeering and abusing. "Chickens. You haven't got the guts, Pakis. Go back to where you've come from."

The next morning, Shabir reported this nasty incident to Jamal Bhai, who suggested that Shabir should start looking for a house and also advised him to buy a car. Now that the shop was running well, they could afford these necessities. A car would be safe for travelling, and a house with a garden would be nice for the children.

In a week's time Shabir had bought a second-hand car.

And the search for a suitable house began.

The house Shabir and Jamal Bhai agreed upon was a walking distance from the shop. It needed minor

updating; otherwise, it was in a ready-to-move-in condition.

Whenever he got the time, Shabir was a do-it-yourself man around the house. He would fix bolts and doorknobs. He would put a shelf here and there in the kitchen or wherever Hina acquired it. He would put hooks on the back of the doors to hang clothes and the like on. He even attached a line from one end to another in the back garden for Hina to put out her washing.

Shabir's neighbour on one side was a West Indian. He was big and black and named Mr White. His wife, Mrs White, was even bigger and blacker. She was a huge mountain of meat. Every bit of her body shook as she walked. She reminded Shabir of a duck waddling. Mrs White's eyes were red, and her lower thick lip was always hung out, giving her a permanent sulky look. Shabir avoided her as much as he could. She always seemed to be scowling and was always kissing her teeth at everything.

Mr White had a son from a previous marriage. The son listened to rap and reggae music at full blast without bothering to close the windows.

Shabir was sick to the throat. The rap songs made it sound as if there were lots of fighting and argument going on in his neighbour's house. Mr and Mrs White screamed at the top of their voices to be heard above the noise of the music.

Shabir tolerated this clamour for as long as he could, but he was at the end of his tether. Even Hina was fed up with the noisy music. Enough was enough, he decided.

He caught Mr White cleaning his front garden and complained about his son.

"Er . . ." Mr White scratched his head and looked sheepishly at Shabir. "It ain't him . . . listening to that music, man. It's me, but . . ."

He good-naturedly promised to take care in future and invited Shabir in for a glass of rum. When Shabir refused, saying that he didn't drink, Mr White leaned on the wall that separated their premises with the broom in his hand and asked Shabir for the recipe for chicken curry. Shabir laughed and told him he hadn't a clue and Hina, his wife, was the better person to ask, as she was an expert in in the kitchen.

Shabir's other neighbours were Mr and Mrs Choudry, and they lived on various benefits. Mr Choudry had started a sort of friendship with Shabir. Every other day or night, Mr Choudry would come to Shabir's house or to the shop to gossip or talk, generally, about politics, England's and Pakistan's present states, and old days back home. Most of all he complained about his daughters.

Mr Choudry had two daughters. The previously charming girls had turned into adolescent monsters. The younger one was under the influence of the older one, he grumbled; they were out of control, trying to behave like the goris and kalis of their school. Why, the other day,

93

he had caught the elder one bunking school with her friend and smoking in the park. He had been horrified.

The daughters, in return, complained to Hina over the back garden fence that their parents were too strict with them. They were denied the little pleasures of life, like being allowed to go to their friends' houses or invite them to theirs, wearing miniskirts, going to the movies in the cinemas by themselves, and so on.

Hina would listen to all this in amusement and then would laughingly report it to Shabir. Hina had led a very sheltered life, and she couldn't understand what the big fuss was about. She had been quite happy with her parents and still maintained a very close relationship with them. She and her family paid each other visits regularly, and she and her sisters were constantly on the phone with each other.

One day, Mr Choudry came to the shop looking agitated, his eyes darting around the shop to make sure no customer was in listening distance. He spotted Mr White at the end of the aisle absorbed in scanning the shelves for something he wanted to buy. Mr White nodded a silent hello to Mr Choudry and went back to his search.

Mr Choudry leaned over to Shabir, who was at the till, and whispered hoarsely, "Don't tell anyone. My eldest daughter has run away."

Jamal, who was stacking cans of juices on a shelf nearby, came over to listen.

"Run away? But where to?" asked the startled Shabir.

"I don't know," said the man miserably, with tears in his eyes. He seemed to have aged beyond his years. "She didn't come home from school yesterday." He made an attempt to wipe his tears.

"Have you informed the police?" enquired Jamal, concerned.

"Yes," said the wretched Mr Choudry. "They are keeping a lookout. They have been to school and have questioned some students and teachers."

The shop's doorbell clanged as a customer stepped into the shop.

Mr Choudry quickly dried his tears and whispered, "Don't tell anyone. I'm ashamed, as it is already in front of my relatives and friends. I don't know how this news leaked out. I will not be able to lift my head up all my life. She has slung mud on our honour."

Shabir felt sad for Mr Choudry. The rest of the day, he and Jamal talked about the incident. These types of cases were common in this country, Jamal Bhai remarked, where East and West was always clashing. The Asian children born in this country were stuck in the middle of two cultures, and they were rolling to and fro like a ball between them.

That night after supper, Shabir went to Mr Choudry's house to comfort him. Mrs Choudry's eyes were red and swollen, and when she saw Shabir, she gave out a clamorous cry.

"Oh, shut up Mum," said her younger daughter scornfully. "She's only run away. She isn't dead, you know."

The look on Mrs Choudry's face clearly said, *I wish she was.* But she shut up. A look of torture passed over her face, and she avoided looking at Shabir. She felt embarrassed. Her daughter had just insulted her in front of him.

Shabir understood the woman's suffering. To distract her he asked, "Any news?"

"Nothing," said Mr Choudry shaking his head slowly.

"Nothing," mimicked his younger daughter. "You don't let her smoke. You don't let her wear skirts, and you don't let her go out with boys. What do you expect us to do?"

The girl was so rude and disrespectful.

Shabir wanted to get up and slap her across the face for her insolence and impertinence. He controlled himself. He wasn't the person to do so.

He felt sorry for Mr and Mrs Choudry and ignored the girl while he was there.

Early next morning, Mr Choudry was at Shabir's house. He looked pale and out of his senses.

"They have found her," he said as Shabir took him to the sitting room.

"They have found her," he repeated. "She had run away with another friend from her school, not a boy as I had dreaded." He looked distraught. "But she won't come back. She's told the police she was kept under restrictions and was mistreated and beaten by us . . . The police believe her and . . . oh, she'll be taken away from us." Mr Choudry wept, beside himself.

What could one do or say in this situation? Shabir felt the man's distress. His own heart was full of sorrow for this man. He had a daughter too. He trembled to think what would happen should she turn out to be like Mr Choudry's daughter.

The feeling of sadness lingered with him all day. Jamal Bhai tried to comfort him. Mr Choudry was lucky, he consoled. Why the other day, Mr Abid's daughter had run away with a kala, and that was a disgrace in itself.

The bell clanged as a kala customer came in.

"I love Asian women," he said as he paid Shabir for a bar of chocolate. "They are so good . . . so faithful . . . and so . . ." He looked around as the bell clanged and the shop's door opened. "And so beautiful." He finished his sentence and winked good-naturedly at Sara Bhabi and Hina, who had just arrived at the shop from the shopping trip they had planned many days ago. They laughed cheerfully at what the kala had said.

Watching this, Shabir thought, *Different gestures have different meanings in different countries. It's how you interpret them.* Take this little incident for instance. In Pakistan, if a stranger had winked at someone else's wife, the husband would have been in a fit, ready to fight the other man. He would have felt disgraced and ashamed, probably blaming the wife for not covering up or encouraging men. And the wife would have been offended by this behaviour from the other man too.

Zainab was trying to catch his attention. She wanted a sweet. Shabir handed her one, love shining in his eyes for her—his dear daughter. She smiled sweetly at him, and his mind wandered back to Mr and Mrs Choudry.

Jamal and Shabir phoned Pakistan at regular intervals. A phone had been installed in their parents' home in Pakistan now. Many times the brothers tried to persuade their parents to come to England to pay them a visit, but they would always refuse gently. They were too old to travel such long distances. And they could not bear to be parted from their two grandchildren (Aslam's boys). Their grandsons were the joy and light of their eyes. Instead, they would request Jamal and Shabir to come to Pakistan.

Shabir yearned to see Pakistan.

He longed to see all his own dear people.

He longed to smell the earth of that country.

He longed to sit in the winter sun and suck sugar canes and eat oranges and peanuts.

He longed to lay on a charpoy at night under the open sky and gaze at the moon and stars.

He longed to hear the the muezzin's five times prayer call that resounded from the mosques.

He longed to walk in the green fields.

He longed to drink that clear water from the well, its wheel driven by an ox.

He longed to go to the *mela* (fair) with his friends.

Oh, he longed for millions of things. And there were millions of things to do here. He needed time. He didn't have time—not even to go to the mosque on Fridays, not even to take the children out anywhere or to pay attention to their studies and help them with their homework. He didn't even have time for himself. Life was so busy here, especially since the shop had opened. Though Sara Bhabi and Hina helped in the shop now whenever they needed to, he still couldn't leave it—not even for a day. He and Jamal Bhai needed each other.

He would go one day though. Yes, he would go and see all those dear people and do all those dear things he longed for.

But until then, he would wait.

Nearly seven years had passed since Shabir had come to this country. The news of his father's death came as something of a blow to him.

Aslam phoned from Pakistan at the shop. Shabir picked up the receiver.

"Shabir Bhai," he lamented, "Aba Ji is dead. Our father is dead."

The news was so totally unexpected that he stood there, faint and weak, with the receiver in his hand. It was impossible. No, it couldn't be true. Why, he had phoned Pakistan the other day. He had talked to Aba Ji. He had sounded . . . How had he sounded? Shabir couldn't recall.

Jamal Bhai came over, and the look on Shabir's colourless face told him that it was bad news.

"He went to sleep last night as usual," Aslam bewailed. "In the middle of the night, he woke up and said he was feeling sick. Me had Ama Ji held him while he vomited, after which he said he felt better and asked to see my two boys. I woke them up and brought them to him. He looked at them for a long time and muttered, 'My Jamal, my Shabir . . . ', and then he smiled and lay down again . . . and stared at the ceiling. I went back to my room with the boys. Ama Ji sat by him all night. In the morning, he was dead. Ama Ji said he had not stirred at all and had died peacefully."

Tears were rolling down Shabir's cheeks. He reached out for Jamal Bhai, and both of the brothers cried uncontrollably.

Both of them wanted to go to the funeral, but of course, it wasn't possible. One of them had to stay behind to run the shop. Jamal insisted that Shabir go, and Shabir insisted that Jamal should go as he was the eldest son; it seemed more proper.

So Jamal went, and Shabir stayed.

Jamal came back, bringing news of the bereaved family, the relatives, and the friends. He had been in time to see his dead father's face. They had buried Aba Ji in the family's burial ground.

Ama Ji looked older. She was beside herself with grief. She wouldn't let anyone touch father's hookah.

Aslam still wanted to come to London. His wife was plump. His two sons were lovely. Everyone said one of them resembled Shabir.

The elder sister was even wealthier now. Her businessman husband was expanding his business. Her eldest son, Munir, was a strong handsome lad now. He was going to America for higher studies.

The second sister had gone sad and quiet since her husband had had a serious heart attack and was ill most of the time. Her daughter was giggly and had eyes for Munir, the eldest sister's son. Perhaps one day, marriage would be arranged between them.

Two more rooms had been built on the roof with the money Jamal and Shabir had sent at regular intervals.

Shabir listened to all this with aching heart.

Time is a great healer. And it healed Shabir's sorrow too. Day by day, the pain of losing his father faded.

Two more years passed.

Usman had taken his A levels. He had no certain goal as to what he wanted to do next. On some days, he would wander aimlessly around, sometimes staying out well into the night. On other days, he would stay in, moaning and brooding.

Jamal, like any ambitious and concerned father, wanted his son to continue his studies. He had hopes of sending Usman to Oxford or Cambridge University.

But unknown to Jamal, Usman had made a blunder that could damage Jamal's high wishes for his son's betterment.

Usman was involved with a Pakistani girl from the next street. And as it usually happens in these cases, the families were the last to find out.

That night, Shabir was at Jamal Bhai's house. Earlier, he had phoned Hina to let her know that he would be home late, as he and Jamal Bhai had some paper work to do regarding the shop.

They had eaten their supper and were sitting down to work when the doorbell rang. Sara Bhabi, on the point of retiring to her bedroom, opened the front door. The girl's father and a few of her relatives stormed in, shouting and abusing, cursing and threatening to kill Usman.

Jamal Bhai's temper immediately went through the ceiling. He demanded to know exactly what all this was about.

"Your son has made my daughter pregnant." The girl's father hurled the earth-shaking bombshell at him.

The explosion rocked Jamal and Shabir's bodies.

"It's a lie," Jamal Bhai managed to say through white lips. But even as he spoke, something in his heart told him that it wasn't.

"Well, why don't you ask him? He has ruined our girl's life," the girl's father raged.

Jamal Bhai went mad. He climbed the stairs like a man out of his mind and dragged Usman down from his bedroom (where he had already heard everything and was pretending to be asleep) and slapped and pulled his hair, demanding the truth in front of the men.

Sara Bhabi stood pale and shaken and watched everything as if in a dream. Not her son. Oh no, not her son.

Shabir pulled Jamal away from Usman and firmly held him by the arms, and to the men he said, "Bhai Sahib (Brother sir) "please go home and take your *chamchas*" (spoons, or side kicks) with you. We'll see you in the morning."

"We won't go till you tell us what you are going to do about all this," one of the relatives said adamantly.

"I said we'll talk to you in the morning," Shabir said in an unyielding voice.

The men left still raving.

"Jamal Bhai, come to your senses. Cool down. This is not the way to treat a young son in trouble. This is not the way to deal with this matter Things can go worse." Shabir soothed Jamal.

"How much more worse can they get?" His whole body shook with convulsive sobs. Shabir felt so sorry for his brother. He found himself at a total loss for words. How do you comfort someone in these kinds of circumstances?

"That bastard has ruined me. All my life I have been explaining our culture and religion to him. And look what he's done. Doesn't the bastard realise that not only has he ruined us and himself . . . ," he gestured with his hand, palm up, at his son, "but he has also committed a sin—a sin for which he'll never be forgiven."

Usman averted his gaze, shifted his feet, and said in a sullen voice, "How was I to know this would happen? She said she was taking contraceptives."

Jamal couldn't believe his ears. Here he was burning, burning, and there was his son, cool as a cucumber, even after the beating. Like a madman, he lunged at the boy again.

But Shabir quickly grabbed his enraged brother and held him tightly with his hands. "What's the use of beating him anymore? He's admitted what he has done. Now we have to think what to do next."

"He'll have to marry her of course," Jamal Bhai fumed.

"Oh no, I won't," blurted Usman. "She can have an abortion."

Jamal Bhai again let out a string of abuses at the boy, cursing him and the day he was born.

"There's nothing wrong with having fun, Dad. Everyone does it. It's just that I've been found out. All my friends do it discreetly," Usman said sulkily.

It seemed to Shabir that Jamal Bhai was going to have a heart attack, listening to his obstinate son. He was panting loudly and was staring at his son in disbelief.

A meek, muffled sound came from the other end of the room. It was Sara Bhabi. Shabir looked quickly at her. She was on the verge of fainting. Bilal and Nazia, who too, at hearing so much noise, had come downstairs, were trying to hold her up. Nazia rushed to the kitchen, brought a glass of water, and put it to her mother's lips.

"Don't you know," said Jamal Bhai to Usman, his voice hoarse from too much shouting, "that you have destroyed the chances of your sister's marriage in a good family—in a respectable family. Who will come for a rishta now?" He buried his face in his hands in despair.

"Don't worry, Dad. No one will find out. I'll pay for the abortion."

It seemed to Jamal Bhai that circumstances were not in his control. The boy had an answer to everything. He couldn't go on beating him. The boy might do something drastic, like leaving home and further damaging his chance of a good life.

"Get out of my sight." You bastard. Get out of my sight and die somewhere with shame—if you have any, that is," ordered Jamal Bhai, completely exhausted.

Usman, with his face red and swollen from the slaps his father had delivered, his usually combed in place hair dishevelled, and his shirt ripped from his father's pulling and tugging, turned and left the room. Though Jamal Bhai had beaten him mercilessly, Usman had not raised his voice or his hands against his father. This much credit he could be granted.

Nazia and Bilal were also dismissed, and left by themselves, the two brothers and Sara discussed what steps to take next.

"There's no point in arguing or denying to the other party. Usman has admitted his offence," pointed out Shabir.

"How about requesting the girl's father for an abortion as Usman has suggested?" joined in Sara Bhabi. "But we must be discreet about everything. That boy has ruined us and himself. Why, he had his whole life ahead of him. We would have married him off eventually. He's too young to carry the burden of a child yet." She started crying.

"Will you shut up, woman?" Jamal Bhai said irritably. "Your tears cannot solve this problem." And he burst into tears himself. After a while, he quieted and said, "I cannot face the girl's parents. I feel ashamed. You'll have to go to them, Shabir."

Shabir held Jamal Bhai's shaking hand in his own. "Of course I'll go, but please don't do or say anything to Usman now."

"What more can I do or say now?" asked Jamal pathetically.

Shabir decided to stay the night. Jamal Bhai and Sara Bhabi were not in the condition to be left alone. He phoned Hina, advising her to lock and bolt all the doors carefully.

The next day, while Jamal Bhai opened the shop, Shabir went home first and informed Hina of the full situation. Then he went to the girl's parents' house and proposed his idea.

"Listen, *Bhai Sahib* and *Behn Ji*"(good brother and good sister), "what's done is done. That's a fact. I and the rest of the family have had deep and long discussion, and we suggest an abortion—"

The girl's mother and father became livid. They cut Shabir's sentence short and demanded that Usman should marry their girl, as her honour had been damaged by him and no one decent would take her for a wife now.

Shabir got angry. They were putting all the blame on Usman's shoulders. It was true Usman had admitted his crime, but wasn't the girl equally involved in it too, he claimed. Usman was at least better than them. He was willing to take the blame but not the whole of it. Why should he?

"Bring the girl in front of me," he challenged, "and ask her why she submitted to Usman's desires. He didn't rape her, of this much I am sure of. Your girl was a willing partner in all this."

The girl's parents, seeing that the situation was getting out of their hands and that they might lose the support of Usman's parents and uncle finally, said unhappily that they would think of this advice.

Shabir insisted on seeing the girl. She was brought in. She was young and looked scared. Shabir felt pity stirring inside for her, but what could he do? He opened his mouth to speak.

"It's all right. I'll talk to her," the girl's mother said hurriedly and explained the intended proposal gravely to her.

"No," screamed the girl. "I won't have an abortion." And sobbing, she ran out of the room.

Shabir came back and reported to Jamal Bhai everything. Jamal Bhai was disappointed. He plunged into depths of depression. He lost interest in everything, including the shop. Sara Bhabi too was under a great deal of pressure and stress and was on the brink of a nervous breakdown. And Usman stayed in his room all day, avoiding his dismayed parents as much as he could.

Shabir hoped that this phase would fade. But as the days passed by, Jamal and his family showed no sign of emerging from their gloom. As a result, the whole household was in a permanent state of melancholy.

Ama Ji was admitted to a hospital in Pakistan. She was in a serious condition. Both Jamal and Shabir were frantic with worry. This was a second tragedy for them, within just a few weeks. First Usman. Now Ama Ji. They both felt they would go mad.

Shabir's heart was pounding as he dialled his parents' number in Pakistan with trembling fingers.

"Bhai," wept Aslam, "Ama Ji is dying. The doctors have no hope for her staying alive much longer. She's asking for you and Jamal Bhai. Please come . . . Don't delay any longer."

Shabir clutched at his heart. Was he going to lose his mother too? No. Dear God. No. Please. No.

He had to go. Jamal Bhai had to go. The shop could go to hell for all he cared. Close it down or let Sara Bhabi and Hina open it. He just didn't care.

Both brothers hectically phoned the travelling agency, but no seats were available till the next week. "Damn it," cursed Shabir. They phoned every airline office they could think of, but their effort was of no avail. It was rush time, holidays time. Sorry, all booked.

The brothers could do nothing but wait now.

This waiting period was the most agonising and painful period Shabir had ever gone through.

He and Jamal Bhai would jump in terror each time the phone rang. Each day, they would phone Pakistan to inquire about their mother, and each day they received the same answer. "She is deteriorating. She wants to see both of you for the last time. Her gaze is fixed on the door."

Shabir hadn't been sleeping for many nights, but tonight he was extraordinarily restless. Two more days to go before their flight. Would time ever pass? It was funny. He had always thought that time passed too quickly here. Why didn't it pass now? His throat felt dry. He must get some water. He got out of bed and made his way down to the kitchen.

He was in the passage when the phone rang. He stood there as if turned to a stone, his heart beating violently. *Oh my God. Don't. Don't let it happen. Not to Mother. I have to see her. Just once. Her dear face, her gentle smiles, her spread out hands in front of Allah after every Namaz* (Muslim prayers, prayed five times daily) *praying for her children. I have to feel her affectionate motherly hugs.*

The phone kept on ringing shrilly, cutting the silence of the night and his heart. He must pick it up. He must. He forced himself.

"Shabir, Ama Ji is dead," Jamal Bhai wailed at the other end. "I've just received a call from Pakistan. She's dead."

Shabir stared dry-eyed at the wall in front of him. So he had lost her then. She had gone. Didn't even bother to wait for him.

"Shabir . . . Shabir . . . Are you there? Shabir . . . Are you ok? . . . Hold on . . . I'm coming." The phone went dead.

Shabir sat on the stairs and buried his face in his hands.

It can't happen. Not to you, Ama Ji. Not you. He rocked to and fro, moaning and groaning, enveloped in grief. And still he didn't cry. *You could have waited. I was coming. I was. Really I was.*

The doorbell rang. He couldn't get up to open the door. He didn't have the strength.

The doorbell kept on ringing. Jamal Bhai had not lifted his finger from it. Hina came out of the bedroom sleepily. The noise of the bell had awakened her. One look at Shabir sitting on the stairs, rocking one side to another, strangled words coming from his throat, and she understood.

Oh my God! She mouthed.

Hurriedly, she came down the stairs and laid a hand on his shoulder.

"Shabir . . ."

He didn't look up. Hina knew grief had knocked his senses out. The bell was still ringing. It could only be Jamal Bhai at this time of tribulation. She went and opened the door.

Jamal Bhai, engulfed with grief himself, went straight to Shabir and saw that he was in a state. He pulled Shabir's hands away from his face. Shabir's face was as white as paper, and his eyes were bloodshot and dry. He was mumbling incomprehensible words.

"Shabir," called Jamal Bhai in an afflicted voice, "cry. You must cry. Let out your grief, or else you'll go mad."

Shabir's eyes and throat were so dry that they were hurting him. "She could have at least waited . . . She . . ." he mumbled.

"Shabir." Jamal Bhai put Shabir's head against his chest. "For God's sake, cry . . ." Jamal Bhai burst into tears.

Still no sound from Shabir.

He held Shabir's face in his hands and said through colourless lips, "Mother is dead. Do you hear me? Our mother is dead. You are never going to see her again. You

111

never said it, but I know you were longing to see her. You can't now. Not ever. Not ever."

This sentence punched Shabir in the heart. He screamed out with pain. Ama Ji had moved beyond his reach. Unbearable. Oh, unbearable. He let out a painful sob.

Jamal Bhai, half dead with grief himself, held Shabir tightly as he cried uncontrollably.

Their last link that had bounded them to Pakistan had been cut off.

Jamal and Shabir had reached Pakistan.

Aslam had come to the airport to receive them. He looked pale and woebegone. As soon as he saw his elder brothers, he flew towards them with tears in his eyes. After hugging them and crying, he said in a grief-stricken voice, "She was all right. She had a few ailments in the past, but nothing major. A few weeks ago, she choked on her food. We took her to the hospital. The doctor checked her and said she'd have to have an operation . . . but she died . . . before they could operate on her. She was asking about you two a lot these days . . ."

Shabir's sigh was full of anguish and remorse. If only he and Jamal Bhai had been able to get the seats to come some days earlier, they would have been able to see their mother's face for the last time before they buried her.

The taxi sped towards its destination from the airport. But no. It wasn't a destination anymore. The rightful owner of that destination had gone. She hadn't waited for them—not even to give a shoulder to her charpoy, which had carried her to her last journey. How unfortunate they were. Shabir's heart bled. *I haven't seen her for the last nine, no nearly ten years now. And I'll never see her again. Oof, these distances-these paths of separations . . .*

The taxi stopped at the main road. They would have to walk the rest of the way to the house through narrow streets.

Shabir didn't look up as he passed Amna's house. But even in his great grief, he knew her door was closed.

A crowd gathered in front of and behind them, and they all walked towards their house as in a procession.

At last, they were in front of their house. Shabir's heart was full of sorrow, and the lump in his throat was getting bigger and bigger.

His mother wouldn't be there to greet them. Oh, what a tragedy! What a catastrophe! How could he step into that house? His feet were laden. It was almost impossible to come to terms with the cold fact that she had gone forever.

An uproar of ululation greeted them. Someone had informed the mourners inside the house of the arrival of the doleful *pardesis* (foreigners).

Shabir put his hands to his ears. This was not the way to greet pardesis. *Ama Ji, look I have arrived. Forgive me for being so late. Won't you come to embrace me?*

113

Both of their sisters came running out of the house, beating their chests and lamenting loudly. They threw themselves at Jamal and Shabir's arms.

"Mother is dead. She was waiting for you." They all wept and wailed and mourned their mother. It was such a heart-rending scene. Two foreigner sons had come from a far-off land to bemoan their dead mother. Every eye was wet at this sorrowful reunion of the brothers and sisters.

As they watched, the crowd whispered to each other.

"That's the eldest son."

"The younger one has come after nine years."

"She died pining for him. The poor woman."

"He married there for British nationality."

"He was engaged to Amna since childhood. You know the one down the street."

"Ah yes. He dumped her, didn't he? Poor girl."

An elderly man patted Jamal and Shabir on the shoulder. "Be courageous, children. Be strong."

A man, probably a distant relative, came wailing down the street, his one arm outstretched. He had just heard of the arrivals of the pardesis.

Someone pushed the crowd away roughly and shouted angrily, "What is this? A *tamasha*" (entertaining show)? "Bring them inside. Are you all mad? Can't you see that they have travelled from so far and are nearly faint with grief? Make way. Let them go into the house. They are emotionally and physically exhausted."

Shabir took a shaky step and entered the house.

Inside the yard, the male mourners were sitting on the *daris* (cotton carpets) on the floor with white sheets spread in front of them. On the white sheets were copies of the Quran, *siparahs* (thirty chapters of the Holy Quran, each binded seperately), rosaries, small prayer books, and stones of dates for counting the recitation. Each of the men came forward, and giving long, sorrowful cries, they embraced and consoled Jamal and Shabir. One by one, they paid their condolences in a heart-moving way. The crowd from outside had come inside with them, watching this sad, tragic scene of sorrow.

"The deceased . . . your mother . . ." (Long wails.)

"Be patient and pray for the departed. That's all there is to do now." (More tears.)

"She was a good woman—a God-fearing one." (Sighs.)

"She wasn't the same since your father died." (All nods.)

"The void she has left can never be filled." (A murmur of agreement.)

"Your mother and father were very much respected in the community." (All conceded.)

"May they rest in heaven." (Muttering of amens.)

Shabir sat with his head dropped on his knees and listened to all this, weeping fresh with each mournful sentence. He had cried so much these couple of days, and still, his heart and eyes were so full. *Ama Ji, Ama ji, where are you? Your naughty son has come home. Come and scold him. Spank him like you used to when he was little. Forgive me for all the yearning I placed in your heart.*

The women were mourning in a separate room. They too were sitting on the sheets spread on the floor. Endless relatives, friends, acquaintances, neighbours again. They were all praying for their deceased mother with prayer books, rosaries, or a *siparah* (one of the thirty chapters of the Quran) in their hands or reciting and counting on date stones. The faint smell of incense lingered in the room. A fresh burst of wailing and lamenting greeted Jamal and Shabir as they entered the room. Both of them took off their shoes and stepped on the sheets. Some of the older women hugged or stroked Jamal and Shabir's heads customarily, while the others just greeted them verbally.

Shabir sat on the floor with them with his head bowed.

"Your mother always helped the poor. She never turned a beggar away from her door empty-handed." A woman sniffed and wiped her nose with her dupatta.

"I haven't slept a wink since she died. I've been so devastated." One dabbed at her eyes. Shabir looked up. He could swear she had some make-up on.

"Your mother was such a *naik*" (virtuous) "woman. She never really picked herself up after your father died. Ahhhhh . . . It' really hard to live without a husband," said a distant aunty, who, Shabir had heard, had recently married for the third time, in an emotional voice.

"I've been praying for your mother's departed soul day and night. And your father's too," another woman said. Her voice sounded sad.

"Her presence will always be missed," said another whom Shabir had never seen before.

He listened to the praise of his mother and father, tears welling in his eyes.

After paying their condolences, the women were talking generally now.

Shabir's gaze went across the room. So many new faces. He hardly recognized them. He looked straight ahead of him and . . . His heart nearly stopped.

Opposite him, on the other side of the room, with her back to the wall, sat Amna. A low table with the incense holder and the Quran on it separated them.

She was covered to the forehead with a thick, heavy *chadar* (shawl). Not a strand of her hair was visible. Her face was pale, as if drained of all blood. Dark circles were under her eyes, and her lips were as white as chalk.

She sat there, right in front of him, eyes downcast, silent and as still as a statue. Only her fingers moved as she dropped the the beads of her *tasbih* (rosary) one over the other in a rhythmic continuity.

He stared at her, wide-eyed, and his heart, which had nearly stopped beating at the sight of her, was thumping violently against his ribs now as if it would break them and jump out and . . . land at her feet.

Not once had she glanced at him. It seemed as if she was unaware of his presence. But how could that be? She—

The women were addressing him.

"Your colour has turned so fair, Shabir," one observed. "It used to be quite dark when you used to be here. And your skin is not blemished as it was here."

Another joined in. "We've heard England's atmosphere is like that. Good for your skin. Good for your health."

"Shabir *putre*" (son), one said, trying to be pleasant, "now that you are here, you must come to my house. After all, I am your aunty. Your dear mother was my sister's sister-in-law's cousin's cousin. I'll invite you to dinner one day. And you too, Jamal putre."

"My daughter keeps pressing me to find a London *wala rishta,*" (suitor from London) "for her. She doesn't want to get married to a boy from Pakistan." A mother boasted her daughter's marriage ambitions.

"It must be wonderful to live in England," another woman said in a dreamy voice.

"It goes without saying."

"Shabir Bhai, you must tell us about England," a young girl chirped.

Shabir felt sick at their hypocrisy. Here they were, mourning the deceased one moment and dying for the news of England the next.

He had seen men, women, and children staring at him and Jamal Bhai in wonderment as if they had landed from outer space. He had seen the longing look—the same longing look as had, indeed, been in his eyes at the mention of London when he had still been in Pakistan.

One woman was saying, "I've heard your wife is very beautiful."

Startled, he looked at Amna. No movement. Not a flicker of the eye. Not an upward glance.

"What's your wife's name?" someone else asked.

He felt confused and embarrassed.

"Hina." His voice was inflicted as he gazed at Amna. No motion. No sudden, shocked hurtful opening of her eyes. No rush of blood on her face. No sign of life. Only the beads of her rosary fell incessantly from her fingers.

"How many children have you got?" another asked.

"Two," he answered in a strangled voice, his eyes still on Amna. The shame and guilt he felt at seeing Amna added more weight, more guilt to his already heavy heart. Amna had not stirred from her position.

He wanted to crawl towards her; bend on his knees in front of her; tug at the hem of her kameez; and, like a child, plead for forgiveness. He could move the table with the Quran on it or crawl aound it to reach her. If only he could . . . If only he could   If only   He got up abruptly . . . and left the room.

Jamal Bhai left for London after two weeks. Shabir was to stay for some more weeks.

Shabir's heart ached as walked around the strangely silent and empty house.

He had longed to come to Pakistan for so long. His thoughts always had happy endings. He would come home. A crowd would receive him at the airport—his father and mother, Aslam with his wife and children, both his sisters with their families, relatives, and friends. From there, they would go home in a procession. His father would tell everyone proudly, "This is my middle son, just returned from London to pay us a visit." His mother would cook food for him with her own hands. How he missed her cooking. Here he was but doing none of the things he had imagined he would do. No sitting in the winter sun. No sucking sugar canes. No walking in the fields with his friends. Nothing.

Time had taken all that away from him. A crowd had gathered, and there had been a procession to bring him home, but it was a crowd and procession he had never imagined—never wanted to imagine.

He entered Ama Ji's room. Her prayer mat was half spread on the floor with Aba Ji's hookah standing beside it. Tears gathered in his eyes as he bent down. Gently, he folded it and laid it on a chair. Lovingly, he stroked the hookah with his hands and put it to one side.

He went into the kitchen. The warm smell of her cooking was gone. All gone.

And gone was the only person in the world with whom you never had to put on an act or pretend.

He was filled with remorse as he thought, *What have I done for all these dear people?* He had left them when they had needed him the most. He had deprived them of their grandchildren. Oh yes, they had Aslam's, but not his or Jamal Bhai's. He had sent them money regularly but had never bothered to ask what they really needed.

He remembered his father—the old man with watery eyes and trembling hands. He had never told his father how much he really meant to him—how much he appreciated and valued him. Why, he hadn't even come on his death. He had been too busy at the shop.

He remembered his mother—his dear gentle mother, coming out of the kitchen, wiping her hands on her dupatta. "My second pardesi son," she had said with quivering mouth. He knew now why she had had that look on her face as she had said goodbye to him. She had known she might never see him again. She could always read him like a book. And what had he done for her? He had given her pain of separation. He had disgraced and humiliated her by refusing Amna. He had let her crave and yearn for him and his children. And had she ever complained? She'd always remembered him in her prayers—always wished for his happiness.

And what had he done for his sisters? Nothing. Nothing at all. He was never there for them. *A'ré*(ho,hey) . . . Brothers are supposed to be their sisters' *maan* (pride and confidants)—someone they can depend on, rely on. Had he ever kept that maan? Had he ever done his brotherly duty? He had hardly ever phoned them or sent them presents to please them, so that they could raise their heads in front of their in-laws and say proudly, "See, that's our brother. He never forgets us."

He remembered once his elder sister had written to him that her bright and brilliant son was going to America for higher studies. She had been so proud of him. She had given her brother the phone number and the address of her son's lodgings. She had asked Shabir to phone him or write to him sometimes, to give him assurance and encouragement, as this was the first time he was leaving home for a foreign country. And what had he done? He had carelessly left the letter lying somewhere, never to find it again. Once the boy, Munir, had phoned him himself. He had promised to return the call and never did. It had slipped from his mind. What kind of *mama* (uncle, mother's brother) was he?

He remembered his younger sister crying and lamenting on the phone that her husband had had a heart attack and was in serious condition, and instead of comforting and consoling her, he had hurriedly told her how sorry he was to hear that while his eyes had been darting at the shop window. He had been too occupied even to listen to her, as the van from cash and carry had arrived and he was in a hurry to have the stuff unloaded.

He remembered Aslam, inviting him joyfully to his wedding, and he had said curtly, "I can't come, yaar. Hina's pregnant. I can't leave her in this condition. And also, we are redoing the shop, so it's not possible for me to come."

And most of all, what had he done for this country? Nothing. This country had borne him, raised him, and all he'd ever done was grumble about it. All he'd ever seen was bad in it. Why didn't he ever find anything beautiful in it? His father. His mother. His sisters. Aslam. Amna. (What had he done? Oh God what had he done?) The trees. The fields. The mud-filled streets. The dirty half-naked children. The passengers sitting on the roof and hanging from the door or sides of colourful decorated buses. The groups of laughing college goers. The young boys playing cricket in the streets or on empty grounds. The muezzine's voice calling for prayers. The moon and stars in the in the summer nights. Why had he been so blind? Why had he been so stupid?

There were so many heart-catching, breathtaking sights. He had never been able to see or appreciate them before.

What would he tell his children of this country? Of his heritage?

The man at the embassy had been right when he had said that, if the students ever returned to Pakistan, they would look down upon the country of their birth. And Shabir had done that too. He had looked down upon the country of his birth.

Shabir was lying on a charpoy on the roof. He had flung one arm over his eyes to protect them from the sun. He could hear flies buzzing in his ears. A child was crying somewhere. A woman was washing clothes in the sun. He could hear her beating the wet clothes with a cudgel to bring out the dirt and make them whiter . . . cleaner.

"*Acha . . . Te janab aithe ne*" (So . . . Your honour, you are here).

Swiftly, he drew his arm away from his eyes. Amna was standing in front of him. Her hair was in a plait, and she had brought the plait around the side of her neck to the front of her kameez. Her dupatta had slipped from her head and was hanging from her shoulder. Her cheeks were rosy, and her eyes glowed.

"Amna." He tried to sit up. "Where have you been?"

She laughed, and her laughter dispersed into air.

"I've been searching for you," she said, her eyes coquettishly slanting sideways at him.

"No, you haven't. You've been busy with other people downstairs," he said petulantly.

"It's you who have been busy with other people." She said accusingly but in a blandished manner.

"Well, so what if I have." Shabir said sulkily. "If you had really been searching for me, you would have found me. I have been here all the time."

"Well, if you don't believe me, I'll go." She turned away angrily.

"No . . . Amna. Listen . . . Wait. Please don't go. Amna!"

"Shabir Bhai . . . Shabir Bhai." Aslam was shaking him.

Shabir's eyes flew open. He closed them at once as the sun nearly blinded him.

So he had been hallucinating.

He was just having illusions.

Sitting up, he gathered his legs and made room for Aslam to sit on the charpoy.

"You were calling out to Amna." Aslam bent his head and looked at his hands. "You haven't heard, have you?"

Shabir's heart jolted. Heard? What? He had heard and seen enough to torture him for the rest of his life. Still with his heart in his mouth, he asked, "What?"

Aslam avoided looking at Shabir.

"Amna's parents married her off after that . . ." He hesitated, struggling with words. He bit his lower lip. "That incident . . . Though her parents tried to hide her unsuccessful attempt at suicide, it leaked out. Her . . . husband came to know of it. He made Amna's life a hell."

Stop, Aslam. Stop. Don't tear my heart out anymore.

"He abused her verbally and physically. If she was quiet, he would slap her . . ."

Stop. Stop. My heart's bleeding. Don't kill me, Aslam.

"And say scornfully, 'Still pining for your *yaar*' (lover) 'Shabir, are you? If she went at his cruelness he'd say, 'No wonder your yaar' left you. You have such a long, miserable crying face.' If she'd ask him for household money, he'd mock, 'I'm not as rich as your yaar. He was right to leave you and go to London. He made his life. What life would he have made here with you?' If he saw her in the doorway, buying vegetables or whatever from a street vendor, he'd drag her in by her hair . . ."

Ahhh, stop shredding my heart, Aslam.

"And beat her mercilessly, piercing her heart with cynicisms. 'I won't have this *badmaashi*' (immorality) 'in my house.'"

Enough, Aslam. Enough. Stop wringing my heart. Ahhh, the pain; it's excruciating.

Aslam swallowed the lump in his throat. (Amna's sorrow was everyone's sorrow). He continued in a pain-filled voice. "Nowadays, Amna is at her parent's. Her husband knew you were coming. He kicked her out, saying brutally, 'Go to your parents' house and meet your yaar to your heart's content.' Amna tolerated all this and still is tolerating. She stays quiet and never complains. But we all know how she's treated. Her parents have begged her to divorce him, but all she says is, 'I've got what was in my kismet, and one cannot fight their kismet.'"

Aslam paused, and his eyes lingered on Shabir's ashen face. "She's punishing herself, Shabir Bhai . . . She's punishing herself for loving you—for trusting you."

Shabir clutched the side of the charpoy so hard that the knuckles of his hands showed white. *Aslam . . . Aslam . . . What have you said? What are you saying? The weight of guilt and shame is already heavy on me. Don't load anymore on it. I beg you. Don't . . .*

Aslam looked straight into Shabir's eyes. "The person most affected by your decision to stay permanently in England was, and is, Amna."

Shabir clenched his jaws and held his head as if in great pain.

Aslam moved to get up. Suddenly Shabir grabbed his hand. He licked his dry lips, and his eyes were filled with anguish. "When I . . . j–jilted Amna, Ama Ji went and . . . Was it . . . was it with your . . . ?" His voice choked.

Aslam looked steadily at his elder brother. "I know what you want to know, Shabir Bhai. You want to know whether, when you refused Amna and Ama Ji went and asked for her hand in marriage for me, she went at my suggestion . . . with my assent."

Shabir was looking at Aslam as if he needed oxygen—life. He wanted the splinter out—the splinter that had been piercing his chest and ripping his heart out. He wanted it out of his heart. Oh, how he wanted it out. It had been goading him for so many years.

"No, it wasn't," Aslam said.

Shabir's grip on Aslam's hand relaxed a little. He could breathe.

"No, it wasn't," Aslam said again. "It wasn't with my assent." His eyes and his facial expression were so truthful that Shabir felt ashamed for ever doubting his brother. He hung his head.

Aslam went on speaking. "I didn't even know Ama Ji had gone to Amna's house with my rishta for Amna till afterwards. I never suggested it. It had never even crossed my mind, but . . ." Aslam stopped.

Shabir's head sprung up. He looked wildly at his brother. *But?*

But?

Aslam gave a quick glance at Shabir and then looked away. "But . . . if Ama Ji had wanted . . . and Amna had consented, I would have married Amna."

Shabir's whole body went limp, and his face went deathly white, as if all breath had been knocked out of him. He looked defeated, lifeless.

"No, don't get me wrong, Bhai." Aslam shook his head. He was alarmed at Shabir's sudden condition. "I had always thought of Amna as your keepsake; it's not as you think . . . ," he paused. "But if I could have righted the wrong you did, I would have done so. I would have done so to keep Aba Ji's, Ama Ji's, Amna's honour. I would have married her and given her a stable home life—would have tried to make her happy . . . and be true to her . . ."

Oh, that hurts, Aslam. Don't hammer blows on my heart. Shabir clutched at his chest. The splinter of doubt was out, but the knife of truth was tearing him apart.

"Amna being dumped by you hurt everybody, including me. I . . . We couldn't bear to see Amna's suffering . . . If she had permitted it, I would have willingly . . . taken your place in her life."

Shabir clenched his jaws and held his head as if in pain.

"Forgive me, Bhai. Forgive me. I know it's hurting you, but I have told you the truth." Aslam stood up and looked silently at Shabir's bowed head, and then he slowly made his way down the stairs.

Shabir sat in the sun and burned and burned in his own fire. There was no water. There was no shade. There was no air.

The forty days of the mourning period were over. Shabir was ready to go back to London.

Aslam's plump wife was smiling at him as he hugged and kissed their children. Aslam stood there watching, the fingers of his hands joining and disjoining with uncertainty. He clasped and unclasped his hands. Should he or should he not? Then he made up his mind that he should.

"Shabir Bhai-" Aslam wet his lips with his tongue. "I wanted to say . . ."

Shabir knew what his brother wanted to say.

"When you get back to England . . . try to do something for me too. I mean, call me over there to settle permanently. Now both Father and Mother are dead, what is here for me?"

Shabir gestured at the house. "This house." He gestured at Aslam's wife and children "Your children Your wife," he pointed out.

"The house belongs to all of us. It's been rebuilt with yours and Jamal Bhai's money. It's more yours than mine. As for the wife and the children, we'll see about them later on." Aslam was adamant.

Shabir looked at Aslam and saw not Aslam but himself, pleading with Jamal Bhai.

"I've talked to Jamal Bhai as well. Wouldn't it be nice if we three brothers got together in one place. This separation is tearing me apart now. I can't bear it any more. You don't know how much I need you two." Aslam was emotionally blackmailing him now.

He sighed and patted Aslam's arm. "Okay. Get your passport and other documents ready. And we'll see what can be done."

Aslam crushed Shabir's hands gratefully in his and hugged him.

"Thank you, Bhai," he whispered emotionally.

Shabir had tried to dissuade him, to disillusion him for so long, but that land was too alluring. No one could resist it. It had cast a spell on Aslam too.

Shabir had said his goodbyes to everyone.

He came out of the house and stepped back to give it a final look. It was a strong house, large and spacious. His children would never come and play in its yard. He didn't even know if he would ever come again himself. Tears sprang from his eyes. Roughly, he wiped them away.

Neighbours were standing in their doorways, peeping from their windows, or leaning over the walls of their roofs for a glimpse of him . . . and to watch him go.

He smiled tremulously at everyone. His friends. His relatives. Some he knew. Some he didn't. His sisters. His brother-in-law. Their children. Aslam. His plump wife. Their children. Everyone.

Friendly, big-hearted people. They were there in your sorrow. In your happiness. They were there when you needed them. While in London . . . No. He shook himself. He really must stop comparing these two countries. It had become a habit with him. Comparing Pakistan to England, England to Pakistan. It was time he broke this habit.

A local porter walked ahead of Shabir and Aslam, carrying Shabir's luggage on his head, which he would load in the hired taxi that stood waiting for them at the main road. Aslam was going to the airport to see Shabir off.

They were walking through Amna's street. The door of her house was open. Shabir wanted to walk past it without looking inside, but his feet refused to carry him. He stood there in front of her open door, rooted to the ground.

A season of autumn hung over Amna's yard. Withered brown and yellow leaves were scattered here and there.

Amna was sitting in the yard on a peerhi in front of the clay stove. Steam rose from the *haandi* (clay pot) on the clay stove. She sat there as still as a stone, her bowed head covered with a thick, heavy shawl.

There was a time Amna could sense Shabir a miles off. But that was a lifetime ago. Today, she was oblivious of everything and everyone.

Then Shabir saw that her hand was moving. And with a heavy heart he realised that Amna was making senseless, oblique lines with a piece of coal on the bricked floor.

Life was strange. You had to pay a price for everything. To achieve something, you had to lose something. And when you had achieved that something, you just sat back and wondered whether it was worth it.

Was all that he had achieved worth all that he had lost? He wasn't even sure what he had achieved or had wanted to achieve. A shop somewhere in the streets of England? To achieve that, he had ruined a girl's life somewhere in the streets of Pakistan.

Oh Amna. What have you gained? Heartache? Pain? Misery?

All she had wanted was his love. His companionship. And what had he given her in return? Rejection. Separation.

His heart contracted.

And . . . suddenly, he was filled with hatred for himself. He stood there loathing, despising, deploring himself. He was abhorrent, despicable, detestable.

He set his teeth.

Get up, Amna, he willed. *Get up, I say, get up. Wound me with allegations. Shout at me. Swear at me. Hurl hurtful words at me. Pull at my shirt. Punch me in the heart. Scream* at me. *Call me a liar. Cheater. Betrayer. Blame me for your ruined condition. Accuse me of unfaithfulness. Of being deceitful. Of disloyalty.*

Lift your eyes, Amna and hate me with them. Reproach me. Confront me. Condemn me. Abuse me. Bruise me. What right had I to play with your heart? Your life? Demand apologies from me. Make me go on my knees. Make me grovel at your feet. Make me beg . . .

Amna, I beg of you. Do something. Say something. Don't kill me with your silence. This burden of conscience, of shame, of guilt is suffocating me, strangling me. Free me from it . . . There he was thinking of himself again. As always.

Amna!

Amna!

Amna!

He willed and willed her to look up, but Amna's will to not look up was even stronger.

Aslam, who had walked a little ahead of Shabir, sensed his brother's absence from his side. He turned around and saw Shabir standing in front of Amna's door, pale as death.

His hands were spread open and his lips were moving soundlessly, as if in a prayer.

Like a sinner pleading for forgiveness.

Like a beggar begging for alms.

Like a dying man longing for a droplet of water.

Aslam understood the suffering Shabir was going through. His heart wept for his brother. And then to his surprise, he saw that Shabir had actually taken a step towards Amna's doorway.

Quick as lightning, he bolted towards Shabir and grasped him by the arm to restrain him from stepping over Amna's threshold.

"Let it be, Shabir Bhai. Let it be. What has happened has happened. Law, religion, and society do not permit you to take this step. You two are forbidden to each other. You two were never meant to be. You shouldn't have stopped here, Shabir Bhai. This is not your destination. It never was. You must walk on—on the path you chose for yourself. Don't turn back . . . You can't turn back. Otherwise, you'll have to bear the consequences. You'll be hurting more people—ruining more lives. It's better to leave circumstances as they are. Leave Amia as she is. You did before . . ."

Aslam's eyes were dissolved into tears, but his voice was strong and clear.

Shabir closed his eyes tightly and bit his lower lip so hard that blood came out of it.

And then he opened his eyes wide and looked for the final time at Amna. She was still sitting there on the peerhi, making senseless, oblique lines on the floor. Time, for Amna, had stood still.

Aslam was right. He must keep on walking. Because walking was life. Stopping was disastrous—ruination

He took a long deep breath and tore himself away from Amna's door.

He was taking with him a piece of autumn from Amna's yard in his heart.

He had left a piece of his soul wandering in front of Amna's door. *If that's of any consolation to you, Amna.*

He boarded the plane that was to take him away from here with heavy steps. And as he fastened his seat belt, the problems he had left back in England came to his mind, jolting him back to reality.

There was still the problem of Usman to be solved.

A search for a suitable boy for Nazia would be on.

The shop was getting too small for all of them. They needed a bigger and more spacious one. Maybe in the high street.

And he had promised to take Hina and the children to Euro Disney this summer.

The man at the embassy had been right. That country had a hold on you. Once you entered it, you were unable to leave it.

It was like an octopus. It clutched you with its tentacles.

DOWRY

Some people were coming to see my daughter tomorrow.

Sakina, who was a distant relative of mine, was bringing these people along. She had praised the boy and the family so much that I was already mentally half prepared for this match.

Sakina, apart from being a relative, was also the matchmaker of our caste. Ever since my daughter had come of a marriageable age, she had been bringing these *rishtas*(matches) on my request-of eligible bachelors that she thought would be suitable for my daughter. None of these rishtas had seriously led anywhere—till now, that is.

It was true my daughter was pretty. She was educated. She could cook, sew, and take care of a house. She was polite and respectful to her elders. I had prepared her well for the circumstances that were to take place in her future life.

It was also true that I was comfortably well off. I had a lovely spacious house, which contained all the basic necessities and luxuries of everyday life—fridge, freezer, cooker, washing machine, TV, VCR, and furniture, to name few. A maid servant came to clean the house every day, and a gardener came once or twice weekly to look after the garden in front of our house.

And it was also very, very true that I could afford a good amount of dowry for my daughter. But that didn't stop me from worrying.

That night, when I talked to my husband about my worries, he gently but firmly told me to put them aside till the boy's family had come and gone. Then, he said, with the grace of Allah, let fate take its course from there.

But I still was not convinced. Deep down, a fear gripped my heart. The fear of my past . . .

I had been jilted on my wedding day.

We were three sisters and one brother. I, Nida, was the eldest. Then there was Bushra, followed by Azra. Our brother, Talal, was the baby of the family, and we all adored him.

We belonged to the lower middle class. My father was a clerk. He had inherited the house in which we lived from his father. So we had a roof over our heads. We were grateful for that, even though the house was badly in need of repairs and paint.

We were always hand to mouth. I don't know how my mother managed to make ends meet, with my father's small monthly wages. It was amazing, but even in those hard times, she'd somehow manage to save bits and bits for my dowry. Through her sheer wisdom, patience, and willpower, she would save enough money to sometimes buy material for *shalwar kameez* (traditional and national Pakistani dress worn by both men and women, loose trousers (shalwar), shirt or tunic (kameez), some crockery, a decoration piece; other times, she'd buy material for duvets, bed sheets, and pillows on which she would ask me to embroider. She had kept her small amount of gold wedding jewellery for us girls. She herself went around without any bangles, locket, or earrings.

She had three daughters to think of. I, being the eldest, was her main concern. We three continued to grow at an alarming speed, which disturbed our parents' peace of mind. We were like a burden on their shoulders, which they longed someone to lift but which they just couldn't throw away.

One day, I was washing clothes in our house yard when there was a knock on the door. We washed clothes by hand and let them dry on the line that hung from one end of the wall to the other in the yard.

I was cold, and I was wet, but I was determined to finish all the washing while the sun was shining. My mother was in the kitchen preparing lunch. She called out out to my little brother, "Talal, go and see who's at the door."

Talal opened the door. From where I sat washing, I could see four women in the doorway. They were all dressed up and looked exactly like women who were out for "match hunting" (looking for girls who would be suitable for their sons). I also sensed they had come for me.

Talal came back and said something to my mother. She hurried out of the kitchen, placing her *dupatta* (a long scarf or stole worn with women's shalwar kameez) on her head. It wasn't often suitors came our way. She went to the door and asked those ladies, respectfully, to step inside. She opened a door that led into a sitting room. It wasn't a much of sitting room really. An old worn-out sofa, some wooden chairs and a centre table was all we had in the name of furniture.

After a while, my mother came out excitedly.

"Nida," she said to me. "Hurry up and make yourself tidy. These women have come to see you. They heard about us from a matchmaker."

To my sisters, she added, "Make tea, girls, and when it's ready, Nida will bring it in."

To Talal, she handed some rupees. "Hurry up and go to the bazaar. Bring something for tea." And with that, she went back into the sitting room.

I pushed the washing aside and stood up from the low stool I was sitting on, grumbling inside. Why did these people have to come today? Why couldn't they have come later in the afternoon or, better still, why couldn't they have announced their visit beforehand? I knew the answer to that. They wanted to catch us unaware so they could see our true states. It helped them to judge our standard of living, financial position, and so on. I wasn't the first girl these types of unexpected visits were happening to; nor was I going to be the last.

I changed into a pink shalwar kameez and dupatta, combed my hair, ran a line of *kajal* (kohl) into my eyes, applied a dash of light pink lipstick, covered my head with my dupatta, and went into the kitchen.

My sisters started teasing me.

Bushra said, "You look nice. They will definitely like."

Azra had a dreamy look. "We'll have so much fun at your wedding."

I felt shy. To hide my red face, I picked up the tray. With my heart beating rapidly, I stepped into the sitting room.

My mother introduced me. "This is my daughter, Nida," she announced proudly.

All heads turned towards me. The two older women were the boy's mother and an aunty. The two younger ones were the boy's sisters.

As I made tea, I could feel their eyes upon me. I felt like a lamb being weighed up by a butcher. I didn't like this tradition but accepted it as a normal part of our lives. This had happened to my mother's generation, this was happening to me, and it would happen to the next generation.

I managed to escape scrutiny of the four women after sitting there for about ten uncomfortable minutes. Once outside, I breathed a breath of relief.

I went and sat with my sisters in the other room, waiting for the unexpected guests to leave. From the window, I saw the two sisters come out of the sitting room. I knew why they'd come out. They'd inspect the rest of the house now. By that, they could judge our financial position and what class we belonged to. Then I knew they would come to scrutinize me even more closely and talk to me, wanting to know if I had a tongue in my mouth and how I would use it. In other words, they would watch my talking manners.

And it happened just as I knew it would.

As the two sisters walked across our small yard towards our room, the eldest glanced inside the kitchen (no fridge, no gas cooker). She glanced at the pile of washed and unwashed clothes (no washing machine). She looked at the home-made soap in a tub on which I, earlier, had been rubbing wet clothes to get the dirt out and then rinsing them by handpump, (no detergent powder, no water taps).

They were in the room now. They looked around (no foam beds, only two *palangs* beds made with wooden frames and knitted in the centre with coarse cotton cloth tapes). Bushra offered them chairs. They sat down. A black-and-white second-hand TV was the only electric device they could see, apart from an old radio and an old iron on the shelf in a wall.

I knew what was coming next, and I was mentally prepared for it. The elder one asked me directly. "Are you still studying?"

"Not anymore," I replied politely. "I've finished my education."

Not deaf and dumb. I could sense her thinking. I didn't blame her. After all, she was looking at me as her brother's likely-to-be wife.

"And how else do you occupy your day? Any particular hobbies or interests?" She hadn't taken her eyes off me.

"I just do housework all day—cooking, washing, cleaning, and the like. When I get the time, I read . . ."

Ah, dutiful, will serve and attend on our household well. I could read her thoughts.

She turned towards Bushra and Azra. "What do you two do?"

"We are still studying," Bushra replied.

A voice called from outside.

"Nargis, Bubbly. Come on; we are going."

The two stood up. "Well, goodbye," said Nargis and left the room with Bubbly following at her heel.

Bushra and Azra started giggling.

We saw our mother letting the match hunters out. Before they left, the boy's mother turned to my mother.

"*Behn Ji*" (Good sister), "you must come to our house," she invited. That meant I had been approved of. In other words, she liked me for her son and wanted us to take the next step that was necessary for this match— the next step being for my family to go and see their son and their house.

My mother replied, "I will talk it over with my husband and will let you know soon."

With that, the women left. I went back to my washing. My mother went back to the kitchen, and my sisters cleaned up the sitting room, chattering and laughing happily.

That night, I heard my mother telling my father about the unexpected guests. After listening patiently, my father said, "This is a matter of our daughter's life. To form an alliance with the other party, we have to inspect and make inquiries about the boy and the family first. Listen, wife. Let's not rush into these things."

But rush they did, or rather, we were rushed into moving with this alliance. It seemed that those people had fallen in love with me. They sent message after message to my parents, inviting them to come and see their son and their house.

Finally, my parents had to give in, and one Friday (being an auspicious day), they set off happily to see the "boy". Of course, Bushra, Azra, and Talal went with them. Nothing could have kept them away.

I was left at home waiting. I wondered what my family would make out of this other family's proposal. Would they like "him"? It was my life, but I had no say in this matter. It was silly really, but come to think of it, it wasn't that bad either. That's the way marriages were arranged in our houses and in our society. I would leave it all to fate. Whatever was written in my *kismet* (destiny) I would get it, and anyway, I knew my parents would decide what would be best for me. After all, they were more experienced, wise and sagacious in life's affairs.

I could see their happy faces as soon as they entered the house. The "match" was definitely on its way.

Bushra threw her arms around me excitedly. "Oh Baji" (elder sister), "Baqar Bhai" (brother Baqar) "is really handsome, and he's educated, and he works on a good post, and they do have a big house and a kept in maid servant, but . . ." She was silent for a moment.

"But what?" My heart skipped a beat.

"Well, it's just that Baqar Bhai's mother seems a bit of a greedy type and a show-off." She glanced at my worried face. "Oh, don't be alarmed. Perhaps I'm just imagining it. Anyway, Ami and Abu" (Mum and Dad) "liked the boy, and your in-laws have proposed for him for your hand in marriage."

I felt shy and hid my face in my hands.

"You will make such a lovely bride," she said.

From then on, it seemed everyone in our house was walking on air. So much happiness abounded that I was afraid. My mother had lost that worried, bewildered expression she usually wore when she looked at us three. I wanted her to stay happy so much that I sent a silent prayer to God. *Please, dear God. Keep her happy.*

The proposal of Baqar was under consideration. One day, some elders from my father's and my mother's side gathered at our house. My father explained the kind of proposal that had come my way. They discussed its ups and downs, while I waited restlessly for the most important decision of my life. They planned my future without consulting me, and I would accept whatever destiny satisfied my elders. I knew they would do what would be best for me. I trusted them completely.

Finally, after much talking, it was decided to accept this proposal. Bushra and Azra, who had been reporting everything to me minute by minute, rushed into the room breathlessly and hugged me together.

"You are going to be engaged in two week's time." They announced in one voice. "Congratulations, Baji."

For a minute, I felt lucky to have someone like Baqar. Then I remembered what Bushra had said about his mother. For a second, a shadow came over my contentment, but I willed it away. *Never mind*, I thought, *I will treat her like my own mother. I will serve her and give her so much love that she'll never regret the day she made me her daughter-in-law.*

With these thoughts, the engagement day drew nearer and nearer. I had not seen Baqar, and he had not seen me. We had seen each other's photos, and that was enough.

My mother went engagement shopping from morning till evening. She bought dress materials for my mother-in-law, father-in-law, two sisters-in-law, two brothers-in-law, and many uncles—and aunties-in-law-to-be. Such limited money and so many expenses. My father, mother, Bushra, Azra, and Talal needed new clothes and new shoes too. Matching glass bangles and artificial jewellery were a must with Bushra and Azra's new shalwar kameezes. I thought, m*y parents are going to spend all their savings on the engagement. What will they do for the wedding?* Deep inside, I felt sad for them, but what could I do? These things had to be done.

Even with these problems, happiness and elation flowed around. The gaiety dimmed a little when my in-laws sent a message that they were going to bring about sixty people to the engagement party. My mother and father went quiet. They could not afford such a large engagement. They had hoped for a simple affair. They could not afford so much food or make arrangements for so many guests.

The elders got together again. After much discussion, it was decided, what difference did it make if so many people came when the proposal was so good? It was foolish to reject such a proposal for such a trivial matter. My father gave in. My heart felt heavy with burden and guilt. I felt sorry for my father. For the millionth time, I wished I was their son instead of daughter.

Friday came. The house was polished and cleaned. Curtains and bed sheets were washed and ironed. Food— salt rice, sweet rice, and meat curry—was being cooked in huge pots outside in the street by a *na'i* (specialist in cooking for weddings, usually from the barbers caste). We were all set to receive the honourable guests.

My in-laws were supposed to arrive at about one o'clock. I had heard they were going to bring many presents for me—clothes, a gold jewellery set, shoes, make-up, a purse, and on and on. Some days earlier, my younger sister-in-law-to-be had come to take my size for clothes to give to the tailor.

I had bathed and sat on one of the palangs in my room. My sisters dressed in bright, colourful clothes, wearing sparkling matching jewellery and bangles, walked around gaily. Talal too was scrubbed and looked spotlessly clean in his new shalwar kameez. Even my mother was dressed in her best cream-coloured clothes. She looked graceful and dignified. I watched her and my father going to and fro, doing this and that before my in-laws came. I felt a rush of love for them.

Some guests from our side had already arrived— relatives, uncles, aunties and cousins, and one or two of our neighbours and some of my friends were also present.

A noise outside announced that "they" had come. My mother hurried to get the mustard oil. She dropped a little for good will on both sides of the threshold before letting my in-laws step in. There was lots of hugging, noise and laughter mixed together. I could hear the word *Mubarak ho* (congratulations) mentioned constantly. My in-laws entered first, and then came the relatives and other people they had brought along, followed by the two servants with the baskets of fruits, sweetmeats, and suitcase containing presents for me. The men were seated in the sitting room, while arrangement for the women was made in the veranda packed with hired chairs.

The dinner was to be eaten in the yard. The hired tables and stainless steel utensils, plates, glasses, and spoons were already laid. Food was ready, and some of the young boys among our relatives and neighbours were ready to serve as soon as they were signalled.

My food was brought into my room by my cousins. I was too nervous and excited with butterflies in my stomach to eat anything. After much coaxing, my friends forcefully but lovingly managed to make me eat some spoonfuls. It wasn't the custom in our families for "the girl" to go out of her room to eat with the engagement guests. I was too shy to go in front of my in-laws-to-be anyway.

After dinner, the yard was cleared quickly. Two *charpoys* (roped beds with wooden rods for frames) were brought in. Someone spread a clean sheet on each one. Our young helpers (boys who were neighbours and relatives) placedsome chairs beside the charpoys. On one side sat my in-laws-to-be with their guests standing or sitting by their sides. On the opposite side, my parents sat with their guests standing or sitting by their sides. Presents were going to be exchanged. My mother-in-law-to-be signalled their servant to bring over the fruits, sweetmeats, and the suitcase. She put the fruits and sweetmeats at one end of the charpoy. Then she opened the suitcase. Everyone went silent and watched.

One by one, she took out five suits for me. Each one was shown to the guests, as was the custom, and placed in the centre of the charpoy. The last one was a red one, beautiful and glittering, with matching shoes and purse. This was what I was going to wear for my engagement ceremony. She opened a vanity box filled with make-up and showed it to everyone. This, too, she put next to the clothes. Last of all, she opened the jewellery boxes. In one box lay a beautiful, pure gold set. In another were six gold bangles and, in yet in another small box, a watch. Everyone's eyes dazzled. There were lots of "oohs" and "aahs" of admirations for these gifts and cries of, "Let the girl's fate be good. May she be blessed by Allah. May she respect and serve her in-laws-to-be and her husband-to-be and lead a good life with them." And on and on they all went.

The red suit, the vanity box, and the jewellery boxes were handed over to my friends. They brought them into my room and locked the door from the inside to. I was ready to be made up.

Outside, my parents were handing out their presents. My mother opened a big bundle. One by one, she took out the clothes.

"This is for the father-in-law."

"This is for the mother-in-law."

"These two are for the two brothers-in-law."

"These two are for the two sisters-in-law."

"This is for the married sister-in-law's husband."

"This is for uncle-in-law number one."

"This is for aunty-in-law number one."

"This is for uncle number two."

"This is for aunty number two."

"This is for . . ."

On she went till the bundle was empty. My mother-in-law had a scowl on her face. She looked displeased but kept quiet. (Later on, we learned that she didn't like the clothes we had bought for them. She said they were cheap and not fit for in-laws of their standard. She had also found faults with the food.)

Meanwhile, inside, my friends were giving final touches to my make-up. Nobody had been allowed to come in while they had been getting me ready. They didn't want to be distracted or have anybody seeing me before I was properly dressed up. Bushra and Azra stood around and watched me being prepared with love in their eyes. I was wearing the red suit, matching shoes, and jewellery my in-laws had brought. My face and hair was made up. My friends gently drew the red glittering dupatta on my head and handed me the purse. I looked into the mirror. I had never thought myself beautiful. But I was beautiful then. I felt and looked like a bride.

Surrounded by friends, I came out of the room. A place was already reserved for me on the sofa in the sitting room. Everyone left his or her place and gathered around me. I was the centre of attraction.

"How pretty."

"Wow! Lovely."

"*Masha'Allah!*" (Allah willed it, may Allah protect from evil eyes, phrase to express joy and praise,)!

Lights flashed. Someone from my in-law's side and a friend of mine had brought her camera. Everyone wanted to sit next to me to have their photos taken.

I was handed some money as a good omen by my close relatives and friends. My mother-in-law took out a wad of notes from her purse and placed it in my hands. She stuffed a bit of *ladoo* (sweetmeat) in my mouth to "sweeten" my mouth. Everyone shouted, "Congratulations," and I was given blessings by the elders.

I was officially engaged to Baqar, without him being there.

Next Friday, my parents, Bushra, Azra, Talal, and some of our close relatives went to Baqar's house. In an extravagant ceremony from my in-laws side, my parents handed Baqar his presents—five suits, a pair of shoes, handkerchiefs, vests, and socks sewn on a towel. They too placed money in his hand.

After the engagement, my parents had thought they would have a year or two's time in which to make the necessary preparations for the wedding. Their main problem was getting the dowry ready.

My in-laws-to-be were in a hurry though. About five or six weeks after the engagement, they started coming around or sending messages that they wanted the marriage date to be set as soon as possible.

My father just would not agree to a wedding so soon. He simply couldn't. Already most of his savings had been spent on the engagement. In a year's time, with any luck, he had hoped to save a little again.

I could see my parents' worried faces every day. In the end, they had to give in, because my in-laws had started an attitude which openly read, *If you don't give us a marriage date now, then we'll look for someone else for our son.*

My father was a respectable man, full of old traditions and values. He had given his word, and it was hard for him to break it. In my heart of hearts, I don't think he was very pleased with this proposal (I could tell he didn't think much of my in-laws, especially their attitude) but good matches were so hard to find nowadays. Parents were forced to settle for matches that were inconvenient and less suitable sometimes.

Once again, my in-laws wanted to bring many people to set the date, but this time, my father had had enough. He just plainly refused. "Not more than five people," he said firmly. "I cannot afford another party."

Again, clothes and sweetmeats were bought to be given to my in-laws. Food was cooked at home on the day. This time, all of my in-laws wore expressions of displeasure.

The date for my wedding was set for three months away. We were breathlessly busy. My father had no choice but to borrow. He was in debt, but that didn't spoil the joyous atmosphere of the occasion-to-be.

My mother kept a cheerful front, though she was worried sick inside. She had so much to think of—new clothes, shoes, and so on for herself, for my father, and for Bushra, Azra and Talal; more people to invite this time; presents for my in-laws and their relatives again; Clothes, shoes and other extra gifts to give to Baqar. A watch and a signet ring were absolutely a must for him on his arrival at our house as a bridegroom at the time of the *nikah* (Islamic matrimonial ceremony). Food with additional dishes of more quantity than those at the engagement were another must.

And most of all, she worried about collecting the dowry. Apart from my in-laws-to-be and Baqar's clothes, my dowry consisted of a lightweight gold jewellery set, fifteen suits (including the one I was going to wear on my wedding day), two sweaters, two shawls, three pair of shoes, one purse, some make-up (consisting of a lipstick, a nail polish, kajal, face cream, a leaf of hair pins, and two clips), some other womanly necessities (two bras and two pairs of underwear), a small amount of crockery (stainless steel and china), some pots and pans and other utensils, one or two decoration pieces, eight bedspreads and sheets, four quilts, a blanket, two towels, and other minor household things, which my mother, God knew over how many years of saving and skimping, had managed to collect. A double bed, a sofa, and four chairs were part of the furniture. It wasn't much, but it was the best my parents could do.

Amidst all the rush, a week before the wedding, a *dholki* (small drum percussion instrument) was brought. Every night, some of my friends and the women and girls among our relatives and neighbours would gather to sing and dance at our house. We heard that there were dholki nights at my in-laws-to-be's house too.

A couple of days before the wedding, the event of *mehndi* or *rasm e henna and tael* (a custom of putting on or decorating the bride-to-be's hands with henna and oiling her hair) took place. The close relatives and guests had started arriving earlier in the evening. The house was full of people. That night was filled with lots of singing and dancing. So much cheerfulness and joyous noise filled the night air that one could hardly hear what the other was saying, but no one seemed to care.

A little later that night, Baqar's family arrived at our place too. They were going to celebrate the custom of henna for Baqar at their house the next day.

I was dressed all in yellow for my mehndi. After dinner that night, held by Bushra, Azra, and my friends on each side, I was brought out of my room and made to sit in a decorated chair in the yard. I spread out my palm. Happily married women, one by one, put a bit of henna on my palm, rubbed oil on my hair, stuffed sweetmeats in my mouth, and gave blessings for this marriage. Everyone sang marital melodies and nuptial songs and danced in rejoicing.

This celebration went on well after midnight. Finally, with everyone utterly exhausted, the custom of henna ended.

The next day, without us realising it, a great big, dark cloud loomed over our happiness.

A messenger arrived from my in-laws-to-be. They were demanding a motorbike in the dowry. My father went into a rage. There was no way he could afford a bicycle, let alone a motorbike. Already, he was in debt, and he wasn't ready to borrow any more. My mother hid her face in her dupatta and cried. Bushra and Azra huddled together in a corner scared. Talal clung to the hem of my mother's kameez, wide-eyed, unable to fully understand what all this was about. Everyone in the house went quiet. Where so much happiness had showered on us earlier on, there was now a dreaded silence. What now? Every one wondered.

I felt like I wanted to die. I was of no value then? The material things were more valuable than me. I felt humiliated and degraded. I was ashamed to face my parents, though it was no fault of mine.

The messenger was sent back without any reply. A rumour that my in-laws were ready to break of the marriage reached us, shaking our entire houschold.

I had never seen my father so upset. He was so angry that we were afraid something might happen to him. "I am giving them the most valuable possession of my life, a piece of my heart. My daughter. What more do they want?" he asked pathetically of the guests who had gathered around him to comfort him.

"And didn't they know that we were not rich. They were not blind. We didn't hide anything from them. If they wanted so much dowry, why didn't they go somewhere else—somewhere where their demands would have been met," he raged.

The elders tried to calm him. The *baraat* (the actual wedding day when the groom and his parents would arrive with their wedding party to take the bride from her house to their house) was due tomorrow. The wedding couldn't be put off. After much persuasion from everyone, he agreed not to do anything hasty, which he might regret later on.

So with heavy hearts everyone went about with the rest of the wedding's final preparations, even going to Baqar's house for his mehndi celebration that night.

Finally, the wedding day arrived. Everyone tried to keep up a cheerful front as best as he or she could. There was a fear in every single heart. It seemed everyone was waiting for something to happen.

By noon, the house was full of guests from our side. The baraat was due to arrive any moment. Food was being cooked outside in our street and a marquee was set up in front of our house. Separate arrangements were made for the men and for the women to sit. Everyone was dressed in his or her best.

I sat in my room on the palang with my knees drawn up, surrounded by my friends. No one was allowed in, apart from Bushra and Azra.

Suddenly a noise arose outside. The baraat had arrived. I waited to hear the music played by the wedding musicians who usually accompanied the baraat. But there was no sound of the wedding instruments. Had they come without the musicians?

My friends rushed outside to watch the arrival of my-in-laws-to-be and their side of guests but, most of all, Baqar, my husband-to-be.

My sisters had filled the plates with flower petals, which they and the other girls were showering on my in-laws.

My mother stood in the doorway with the bottle of mustard oil to pour on both side of the threshold for good omen and garlands to put around my in-laws necks before they entered our house, while the men of our house stood outside in the street to receive the honourable guests.

My in-laws had brought a large party—nearly two hundred people—another burden on my poor father. Would there be enough chairs for everybody to sit on? Would there be enough food to go around? We all wondered.

My friends came back, chattering and giggling.

"Your bridegroom's really handsome," they said. "And he's arrived in a decorated car, not on a horse." (Traditionally, some bridegrooms preferred to come on horses.) "He's wearing a suit, but he hasn't tied a *sehra*" (groom's floral chaplet) "around his head."

Feeling shy, I hid my face on my knees.

"But there's no *band baja*" (accompanying wedding music). "The baraat doesn't seem right without music," one of my friends moaned.

"I wonder why they haven't brought the musicians?" the other one asked, a bit surprised.

I had no answer to that.

Bushra and Azra were still outside, probably giving milk to the bridegroom and maybe arguing over the money they would receive in return from him. It was only a part of the fun—another happy tradition.

They both came back, looking dejected.

"How much money did you get for *doodh pilai* (milk drinking ceremony when the bride's sisters, cousins bring milk for the groom, after drinking he presents them with money)?" my friends asked them eagerly.

"Nothing. Your mother-in-law and sisters-in-law have swollen faces, Baji. Don't know what's wrong with them," they complained.

Outside the two na'is and the helpers (again young boys from among our neighbours and relatives) were waiting to be told when to serve the food. Mine would be brought inside.

By and by, we heard that a serious conversation was going on between my parents and my in-laws-to-be. Next we heard that the conversation had turned into a heated argument.

I sat in my room and dreaded what was going to happen next. I glanced at my beautiful glittering bright red, ready-to-wear wedding clothes. They seemed to be laughing at me.

The ceremony of nikah (Islamic matrimony) was going to take place now. The n*ikah khawan* (Muslim priest to perform matrimonial rites) arrived with a register in his hands. Baqar's matrimonial rites were going to be performed outside separately, watched by his and my elders after mine had been completed. I bowed my head so the dupatta fell over my face and half hid it. The nikah khawan recited some verses of the Quran and asked me to repeat after him. Then he asked me if I would accept Baqar Ahmed, son of Fazal Ahmed, as my husband and the standard *haq mahr* (dowry money settled upon the wife from the husband) from Baqar.

The thought that, from now on, my life was someone else's came to my head. I would leave my dear parents and this house for some unknown, strange people. I did not know their ways or their natures. They were the people with whom I was going to spend my life from now on. I already thought of them as my own future people, but would they accept me wholeheartedly too? There was no doubt at all that I would adapt to their way of life and adjust myself with them come what may, but would they be as cooperative with me too, accommodate me as one of their own? My thoughts prolonged. The nikah khawan urged.

"Say yes, daughter, and then sign this form here." He handed me a pen.

I was about to say yes and sign the marriage deed when a woman relative dashed in. "Stop, m*aulvi sahib*" (honourable priest), "stop." She panted. To me, she said, "Don't say yes or sign, daughter."

My head flew up. I went pale as the woman informed us, "There's a dispute outside between both parties. You had better come out too, maulvi sahib."

The nikah khawan gathered his register quickly and hurried out with the woman. Bushra and Azra raced after them. I stared at my friends in confusion. They were equally confused. In my heart, I knew what had happened. The dowry . . .

My friends rushed outside. So did all the guests that had gathered around me to watch the Nikah ceremony. I was left alone. My feet felt as though they were chained, but somehow I managed to drag myself to the window. In the yard, through the crowd, I could just about see my in-laws and my parents. There was a heated accusation from my in-laws about my dowry.

"Why didn't you fulfil our demand? We only asked for a motorbike, not a car. We didn't ask for ourselves. It would have been used for your daughter too. It would have been handy for Baqar to take her around."

"But," one of our elders tried to reason with them, "We didn't ask for a large amount of haq mahr from your people for our daughter. We were satisfied with what you agreed to give her for this jointure."

"What do you mean by that?" my mother-in-law inquired angrily. "What about the expensive *vari*" (wedding gifts to the bride from the groom's side), we have brought for your daughter? Is that nothing?" she asked sarcastically.

"*Behn Ji*" (Good sister), "our daughter is your daughter now." Another of our relatives tried to cool the situation down. "Let us leave this kind of talk and celebrate the wedding with happiness."

"Oonh! Happiness?" My mother-in-law jerked her head as if in disgust. "What happiness? You haven't left anything for us to be happy about. You people have not honoured our wish. You have shamed us in front of our relatives. A little wish of ours, and you people couldn't comply."

And so, on and on it went, until it got to the point that my in-laws were ready to take the baraat back.

Through pain-filled eyes, I saw my father, my poor dear father, joining both of his hands together, in a gesture of imploration, for my sake, in front of those cruel hard-hearted people.

"I can't afford a motor bike yet," he begged. "But I promise you, after the wedding—"

His words were cut off. "You haven't even given any electric devices in the dowry now. How will you be able to give a motorbike then?"

The tears of desperate, helpless parents, who had three daughters, did not soften these wealthy but mean people's hearts.

The bridegroom, an onlooker in all this, stood as though he didn't have anything to say in this matter, as though this dispute was no concern of his. I could only see a part of his face, and at that moment, I hated him. I hated him and his family for causing so much sorrow for my loved ones.

His furious mother turned to him now. "I'm leaving. If you want to marry, you'll marry alone, without any of us by your side, without my permission. There's no way I'm going to stand here and watch you marry into this household. We haven't been appreciated. We have been disgraced and humiliated. You too . . . Think, Baqar."

With that, she marched out of our house, followed by the rest of her family.

Baqar hesitated a moment. He looked at my father's joined hands. He looked at my mother's and father's pleading eyes. He looked at the window of the room I was in. He looked at his mother and father walking out. He decided to follow them.

I heard a wailing scream. It was my mother. She had fainted with grief. Women hastened to attend her. I saw my father being rushed to the hospital. He had nearly had a heart attack. The guests that had come with my in-laws had already left. Only the guests from our side remained. My sisters clung to each other and wept in anguish. Talal kept hugging my unconscious mother and sobbing, kept calling, "*Ami, Ami, utho*" (Mother, Mother, get up). The house that had been filled with happiness some moments ago had turned into a house of mourning. It was as though someone had died here.

My friends came into my room, sorrow written on their faces. Somehow, they moved me from the window. They rubbed my cold hands and feet. I was in a state of shock. I stared ahead with dry empty eyes. I could not cry, could only stare at people who came in now to pity me, console me, or comfort me.

"Ah, poor girl," I could hear them say, and I could feel their pity.

"Cry, daughter, cry," an older woman said. "If you don't, you'll go insane." She turned to the others. "Find a way to make her cry."

They shook me and slapped me. Still I did not cry, while everyone around me cried.

By night most of the guests had left. Only the close relatives stayed. So much food was wasted. No one could bear to eat.

My sisters came and took me to see my mother, who was lying in the next room. She was conscious now. As soon as she saw me, she took me in her arms and cried and cried. Then I cried too.

So life went on. My father came back from the hospital, miraculously alive. He and my mother went around with bowed heads. My sisters were quiet. Their constant laughter and chatter had died. Even Talal was not his usual cheeky self like before. As for me, I was a walking corpse. I watched my family and died a thousand times every day. They were punished, though they had not sinned; nor had they committed any crime. *Dear God, Why?* I asked over and over again. Why was I born a girl? Didn't I have any price? Was dowry more important than me? Were material things more valuable than me?

Within time, a couple of rishtas came for me, but when they learnt that I had been jilted on my wedding day, they retreated. People talked and then forgot about me.

One day, a very reasonable rishta came. These people came for me, but instead of choosing me, they chose Bushra. They wanted nothing but the girl. The suitor was an engineer. They were well off, and most of all, they were not dowry hungry.

My parent's heads bowed even more. They wouldn't meet my eyes. Where was the fairness of it all? The eldest daughter still sitting at home, while the younger one would be married first! No. They wouldn't hear of it, so they refused the proposal for Bushra.

The silence in the house was unbearable. Life had to turn back to normality. Could I be the one to break this abnormality and bring everyone back to sanity? Could I be the one to erase some of the sadness that had befallen this house and bring back some sort of joy into it? Well, I was going to try. What had happened was my fate. Why should Bushra be punished for it?

I came out of my grief, and for the first time in my life, I spoke to my parents about these matters. I said, "What has happened has happened. We cannot change that. Think of your other two daughters instead of thinking about me all the time. Please don't refuse this proposal that has come for Bushra. Another one like this might not come again, so why not grab this golden chance? I'm sure everything's going to be all right this time. There will be no rejection but acceptance this time. Bushra will be luckier than me. Please agree to it. Secure it. Give your consent to it. Don't let Bushra's time and age pass because of me. I will never be able to forgive myself if that happens."

My parents wept. They opened their arms, and I buried my face in their chests and cried along with them.

Bushra got married. Her in-laws kept their word. They wouldn't accept any dowry, but my traditional father, committed to customs and usage ways, wouldn't dream of marrying his daughter and letting her go to her in-laws' house empty-handed and arranged whatever little he and my mother could for Bushra's dowry.

The wedding took place, and once more laughter returned to our house, though the air was heavy with sadness.

More time passed and would have kept on passing if Javed hadn't come along—like spring after autumn.

I had never let anyone know about my feelings for Javed. Long ago, whatever I had felt for him had been buried in my heart. He was my cousin. His mother was my father's sister. He was her only son, and they were very, very rich. They were counted as one of the richest families in town. He was like the moon to me. Unreachable. Unattainable. I knew it, so I had faced reality. He could never be mine. I had pushed my love for him into the depths of my heart.

Being a cousin, he used to come to our house. His behaviour to my parents was respectful and loving. He laughed and talked with my sisters but hardly ever paid any attention to me. I didn't know why. He would never look fully at me. I would watch him secretly and memorize all his moods, expressions, and gestures . . . his way of talking, laughing, smiling, the way he turned his head, the way he raised his eyebrows, the way he walked were all imprinted in my mind.

Then he had gone to America for higher studies. He was even more out of reach now. I had gathered all his memories and locked them in my heart, like something valuable, precious, to be cherished.

I had never, ever imagined, even in my wildest dreams, that he could ever be mine. So when Javed's proposal came, I was thunderstruck to say the least. I knew for sure his request for my hand was out of pity, and I didn't like that and suffered.

My *phuphu* (aunty, father's sister) arrived one day and asked for my hand for Javed. My parents were stunned. For a while, they were speechless. They stared foolishly at my aunty, as if unable to comprehend what she was saying.

"Saleema," my father whispered emotionally. He couldn't speak. Did opportunity, fate knock on your door like this?

She had always been there, his sister—the rich wife of a wealthy businessman. Bungalows, cars, servants, foreign trips, money—she had everything. And though my parents knew she had a grown-up son, they had never dared to hope or even think about my match with him. Not even before Baqar's rishta had they entertained that notion. And if they had, they'd never mentioned it to anyone, not even to each other . . . not even to themselves. They knew their position, their status. My aunty and Javed were always there but never for them.

Phuphu Saleema took my father's hand in her hands. "Yes, *Bhai Jaan*" (dear elder brother). "I understand what you are feeling or what you might want to say. I knew you had three daughters, and I was also aware of your helplessness. I had thought a hundred times of lightening your burden by asking for Nida's hand in marriage for Javed—not because I felt sorry for your meagre circumstances but because I really thought Nida would make a wonderful wife and a wonderful daughter-in-law. She had all the qualities of a homemaker. She would have brightened any house she would go to. A pretty, educated, mannerly girl, who respected her elders, but most of all, she was your daughter. What more could I want? But Javed had never given me a slightest sign or a hint that he was interested. Then he went to America. I thought, in time, when he finishes his studies, returns to Pakistan, and finds a job, I'll talk to him. Unfortunately, I left it too late. Nida got engaged. I thought, Allah's will; perhaps it was for the better. So I stayed quiet. Then we all know what happened at the wedding. I wanted to stand up right there and then and shout to those cruel, callous people. 'Go if you must. Nida's not a fallen girl. I'll make her my Javed's wife. I'll show you. I'll take her empty-handed with respect.' Bhai Jaan, you don't know how I longed to say these words, but I stayed silent because of Javed. I cried along with you, unable to do anything for you, feeling powerless, but now Javed himself has sent me. You don't know how happy I feel. At last I can do something for you, dear brother. I always wanted Nida for my daughter-in-law."

My father, mother, and aunty had tears in their eyes.

"Does Javed know about Nida's past—that she was jilted on her wedding day?" My father wanted nothing hidden from Javed.

"Yes, Bhai Jaan, he does. And he doesn't care one bit for the dowry or what people say and think. We have everything by the grace of Allah. Just give us your daughter."

So in a simple ceremony, I was married to Javed. Sometimes, the moon did land in your lap of its own will. I still had a doubt in my heart. Did he marry me out of pity? And I got the chance to ask him that question on the wedding night. He held me tightly in his arms and answered, "I don't pity you, but I do pity those people. They don't know what they have missed. They have let heaven slip out of their hands. I hope they rot in hell now."

With my face hidden in his chest, I told him of my memories of him.

He laughed and said, "Did I really do that? Maybe I was scared of being romantically involved with you. You are a kind of girl one can easily get involved with. I guess I was scared of being committed. I don't know why, but it's the honest truth."

So my feelings weren't entirely one-sided. He had felt something too. I felt my spirit being lifted.

"Supposing I had gotten married to Baqar," I pointed out.

But my husband refused to take this point seriously. "You were meant to be my fate, so how could your marriage have taken place to anyone else? And now I'm going to love you for the rest of my life."

And he did. He gave me love and happiness and everything I could wish for. He gave me a reason for living.

We had a great and grand *walima* (reception, held after the wedding day, when the groom's family invites the bride's family and guests tp publicize the marriage). A wedding wouldn't be complete without that. Years later I could still, in my mind, see my parent's rapturous faces that day.

I slept then and woke up at dawn. The muezzin was calling for prayer. I looked at Javed sleeping beside me and then I got up, performed my ablutions and said my *Fajr Namaz* (morning prayer).

A new day was beginning and I was ready to face it. I went about the house with a light heart, making arrangements and preparing food for the important guests who were coming to see my daughter for their son a bit later in the day.

As I stood in the doorway to receive them, a prayer arose from my heart, *Please, dear God, let no girl be rejected because of the lack of the dowry,* I prayed. *And even if you do send some Nidas into this world then don't forget to send some Javeds along too.*

And welcoming the guests into my house whom, Sakina, the matchmaker, had brought along with her, I felt what my mother would have felt.

REAL

Dadi (grandmother, father's mother) didn't like Kanwal's ways one bit.

Ever since she had come to London, she was seeing that Kanwal's habits and manners had somewhat deteriorated and her actions were not very agreeable or acceptable. Western colours had dominated her. She was very much influenced by this society here.

Anyhow, that wasn't really that surprising. Anybody living in this country would accept some of this influence, and Kanwal was a product of this country and society after all. But that she would be coloured in their colours and affected in Western ways to such an extent was what was rumpling Dadi's mind.

Dadi noticed that Kanwal never wore *shalwar kameezes* (traditional Pakistani dress worn by both men and women, loose trousers (shalwar) long shirt or tunic (kameez) and was in jeans and a short skimpy blouse all the time. She chewed chewing gum like a cow ruminating continuously.

Dadi never heard the words "Aslaam o Alaikum" (Peace be upon you, Muslim greetings at seeing someone) or "Allah Hafiz" (Muslim farewell words, goodbye, may Allah protect you) from her lips. Only words like "hello", "hi", or "see you" came out of granddaughter's mouth.

Dadi saw she came home late at night from university, even though the university was only about an hour away from her home.

She was not interested in doing any work—neither housework nor work outside.

She never sat down with the other members of the family to eat at home and did not talk to them much.

When she was home, she'd mostly stay in her bedroom, chatting with her friends on her phone or sitting in front of the computer. Every minute, her phone would ring or she would be ringing, and at the sound of the beep, she would instantly read the text and then would instantly reply to it, as if it was a duty that she had to do.

On her day off from university, Kanwal would get up late in the afternoon, have a bath, come down to the kitchen, make herself a cup of tea, and take it upstairs to her room, where she would listen to English songs at full volume or talk non-stop to her friends on her mobile.

At about four or five, she'd run down the stairs with loud thuds and call out "bye" while she still on the last step and rush across the passage. And with that, there would be the sound of the front door opening and closing with a bang behind her.

If her friends phoned on the house number (which was rare), they'd say, "Can you please call Kono?"

Dadi would set her teeth.

Sataya naas! (Ruiners!) Fie upon these friends, who had ruined such a nice lovely name like Kanwal by changing it to Kono.

And . . .

Dadi had never once seen Kanwal reading N*amaz* (Muslim prayers, prayed five times daily) even though her son and daughter-in-law were profoundly committed to praying five times a day and fasting in the month of Ramadan. Even living in London, they were deeply connected to their religion and their Pakistani customs and usages and culture.

Dadi had acquainted all of her own children well, not only with worldly education but religious education too. Maybe that was the reason Kaleem (her son) and Farhana (her daughter-in-law who was also from a similar background) had never forgotten those customs and traditions.

Apart from English, Urdu and Panjabi were spoken in their house. English and Pakistani food was cooked. Aside from English friends, Pakistani friends, relatives, and acquaintances came and went.

In Kaleem and Farhana's bedroom, as well as in the sitting room downstairs, she found CDs of Pakistani film and non film and *ghazal*(poetry) singers such as

Noor Jahan, Mehdi Hassan, Masood Rana, and Naheed Akhter, and of *qawals* (devotional singers) like Nusrat Fateh Ali Khan, Aziz Mian, and others. Her son and daughter-in-law also had DVDs of many old Pakistani films and comedy stage dramas in the house. They went to see Pakistani and Indian films in the cinema occasionally.

Asian radio stations broadcasting from London were listened to. Farhana was especially fond of tuning into the Pakistani or Indian radio while cooking in the kitchen or while driving in the car.

In addition to English TV channels, Urdu, Panjabi, and Hindi channels were subscribed. Pakistani and Indian dramas, films, and programmes were very popular with everyone in the house. Urdu news was seen. Urdu newspapers and magazines came to the house.

Naats (encomiums of the Holy prophet), *Hamd* (praises of Allah), and *Kalam e Pak* (recitation of the Holy Quran) were listened to avidly by the whole household. Qari Waheed Zafar's Naat "Allah Hoo" ("Allah Is True") was a favourite with the entire household. The names of Allah and Mohammed PBUH were framed and hung on the walls of the house.

Kaleem never missed a Namaz, not even at work. On his days off, whenever he could find time, he would go to the mosque near their house for Namaz in a congregation, especially the *Juma Namaz* (Friday congregational prayers). And sometimes, Farhana would have ladies' *Quran Khawani* (reading of the Quran) in the house.

It wasn't as if Kanwal had no idea of the customs and usages of Pakistani ways or had not had any Islamic studies. She had been taught about her religion. Her parents had made sure she had learned Namaz and the Quran at an early age, and they had taken her to Pakistan few times to make her observant of the culture there. Living in a very British Asian Muslim environment at home and still being overpowered by the influence of Western culture . . . ?

Dadi was truly baffled.

Kaleem, after much persuasion and coaxing, had made Dadi agree to come to London; otherwise, she wouldn't have been willing to leave her home at her age. She didn't know when the call from above would come, and she wanted to wait for the invitation from heaven there in Pakistan and be buried in the chaste soil of her own country.

And now, compelled by her son's love, she had come here to stay in England with his family for some time. Dadi had brought up all of her offspring with a very cultured observance of rules and etiquette. She had profusely filled all her children with the love of their country, their religion, their customs and traditions, and family values. Aside from giving them a first-rate education, she had made sure they were equally well educated about their religion.

When Kaleem had come to London for further higher education, Dadi had given him a hundred pieces of advice before sending him here, advice that Kaleem had tied to the hem of his heart.

After finishing his education, he had found a very good job here. He had, for the sake of his livelihood, decided to stay here permanently.

She had already thought of a good *rishta* (match for marriage) for Kaleem. He was obedient anyway, that's why he had bowed his head in front of his mother in a sign of respect and consent. He had full confidence and faith in his mother, and this confidence and faith had made his married life a success.

Farhana was a beautiful, virtuous, educated girl. Respecting her elders and treating her juniors with love and making places in elder people's hearts by being dutiful and serviceable were skills in which she was well accomplished. With these good habits and well-mannered ways, she had won the hearts of her husband and mother-in-law.

Dadi's disposition was so majestic and awesome that anyone who ever saw her became awestruck. She had a commanding and domineering personality anyway. Nevertheless, she loved Farhana even more than she loved her own daughters.

Even while living in London, Farhana had kept the atmosphere of her home in a purely Asian way, but still, she and Kaleem were not in the mind to prohibit or restrict their children unreasonably. They wanted to see their children full of confidence in every turn of life.

That was why, to make Kanwal observant of the culture, environment, and mode of life there, they had taken her to Pakistan few times with them.

Kanwal had like Pakistan very much.

The sincere sociability of the people there . . .

The fragrance of the earth in the air there . . .

The lively, crowded, and busy bazaars there . . .

The wrangling, haggling, and arguing women over the price of goods in the shops or stalls there . . .

The sitting in the winter sun on the roof, eating oranges and peanuts . . .

Buying *chaat* (spicy sweet dish of chickpeas and boiled potatoes with yogurt on top) from a street vendor . . .

Kanwal had loved all that.

And Dadi's matter was something really incomparable.

Kanwal had once been passionately devoted to her grandmother. And now the girl wouldn't hear of goint to Pakistan and her passion for Dadi had faded.

How much difference there was between Kanwal and Sunbul.

Now take Sunbul for instance. Like Kanwal, she had been born and bred in London. She'd grown up here, but she was attached to the Pakistani culture and customs and ways. She liked wearing shalwar kameez. She liked talking in Urdu and Panjabi. She spoke in a soft well-mannered tone. She had mostly Asian friends. When the time for her marriage had come, she had left it all to her parents' will. She was beautiful and could have chosen any boy for a husband for herself, but she was in the favour of arranged marriages. She had seen that arranged marriages were more successful and that parents were more far-sighted, sagacious, and shrewd in these matters. She had left the decision of her life with her parents. Ahmer's proposal was extremely reasonable. He was from a good, educated family. After marriage, Sunbul had called him over from Pakistan, with his parents' consent. He had a good job and had settled well here. She and Ahmer were sharing a very successful life. And now, she had a lovely little boy who was adored by everyone in Kanwal's house.

And there was Hamid too. He and Fatima were leading a happy life. Certainly, they had married for love but with their parents' consent and blessings. When Hamid's marriage was mentioned in the house, he had, in a restrained voice, told his parents of his choice.

Fatima was originally from Algeria. She worked in Hamid's department. The whole of the staff in the department was English. Being Muslims, the friendship between Hamid and Fatima had progressed from hello, Aslam o Alaikum to love.

Profoundly dark-skinned, Fatima, whose big, big eyes were always loaded with kohl (lamp black collyrium), didn't use any other make-up at all, but still, how very attractive she was. How lovely she looked while speaking sentences in broken Urdu and Panjabi.

Hamid and Fatima's house was not very far away. Every evening after work, both of them would come to say *Salaam* (hello, salutation) to Dadi and to meet the rest of the family.

Wearing a full length gown over an ankle-high skirt and full-sleeved blouse, with a scarf covering her head all the time, that graceful dignified girl, Fatima, who did not hail from their country, still seemed so very their own. And when she said "Aslam o Alaikum" or "Allah Hafiz" in her Arabic accent, inebriated Dadi from the inside.

Once while reading a naat in Arabic, Fatima lodged into Dadi's heart as water lodges itself into the roots.

Fatima adhered to praying five times a day. For her daughter-in-laws wedding, Farhana had beautiful Shalwar kameez sewn for her. Sometimes Fatima wore them, but she still covered herself with her over gown and wore her scarf on her head. She treated all the family members with the utmost respect. Dadi would go *sadké waari* (someone asking God to accept them as a votive offering and protect the one they love) over Fatima and expressed extreme affection for her and, with every glance, favoured her with love. She made propitiatory offering and prayers to ward off evil eyes from her grandson's wife.

And there she was—Kanwal—the exact opposite of the rest of her family.

At first, Dadi just watched her granddaughter's wayward manners and style of living. Then, compelled by her heart, she started giving Kanwal advice or telling her tales of her own experiences.

And Kanwal did listen, but as soon as Dadi left the room, she threw her grandmother's words out of her ears.

Toba! (Heaven forbid!) How outdated were Dadi's thoughts. She was trying to make her comprehend the highs and lows of life as if she was a child. Well! She could take of herself.

It wasn't as if Kanwal didn't love Dadi or that she wasn't happy that Dadi had come to visit them. She loved Dadi a lot, but she was terribly irritated by Dadi's advice, counsel, and instructions. Anytime she sat with her grandmother, Dadi would open bundles of advices. Sometimes, she'd tell her a *Hadiss* (a narrative or tradition of the Holy prophet). Other times, she'd give examples of the other apostles or messengers of God. Sometimes, she'd narrate stories and tales with lessons in them. And still other times, she'd tell Kanwal her own experiences of life and how this world had become corrupt, scaring her by painting a picture of how much bad happened in this world these days.

Lectures! Talks! Advices! All the time. Kanwal was bored stiff with Dadi instructions and admonitions. As a result, she started pulling away from Dadi.

And what happened that day exceeded Dadi's limit.

It was a day off from work. Kaleem had gone out somewhere. Farhana was in the kitchen, and Dadi, as usual, was in the sitting room reciting, with a *tasbih* (rosary) in her hand. Her mouth kept moving silently in the glorification of Allah, and the beads of her rosary slipped one after another in a rhythmic motion through her thumb and finger. Her face looked very *noorani* (resplendent or saintly) in her large, white *dupatta* (long scarf or stole to go with women's shalwar kameez). She was completely engrossed in her recital. The horn of a car broke her absorption.

How rude! Who was this unmannerly person? She didn't know. You didn't hear many car horns in this country.

Dadi ignored the interruption and started reciting again. The horn blew again. It had become difficult to recite now. She lifted the curtain of the front room's window and peeped outside. A car was parked on the road in front of their house. An Asian looking boy was sitting in the driver seat with his hands on the wheel. He was blowing the car horn so much that a *kala* (black man) from the upper story of the house opposite them, opened his window and, pushing his head out, screamed aloud, "Hey, shut it, man, or I'll come down and bash your head in."

The boy came out of the car and stood on the road with his chest out. He lifted his face up at the kala and screamed back defiantly, "Come on then; try it."

The kala swore loudly and slammed the window shut. Probably he was coming down on the road to fight.

In the meantime, Dadi heard Kanwal's loud footsteps thudding down the stairs.

"Bye, everybody," she called out from the last step of the stairs, and with that, Dadi heard her rushing through the passage, opening the front door, and then slamming it shut behind her.

Dadi saw that Kanwal had reached the car, and the boy who had gotten back in the driving seat, was leaning over and opening the passenger side of the door for her.

Kanwal jumped into the passenger seat while saying, "Hello, hi", and the car moved forward instantly.

Dadi's blood started to boil.

So much shamelessness—immodesty!—and so openly.

Were her son and daughter-in-law blind?

She was shaking with rage and anger and becoming a figure of ire and fury, she went into the kitchen to her daughter-in-law.

"Farhana," she called out aloud.

Farhana was sitting at the kitchen table cutting vegetables with a knife. On hearing her mother-in-law roar, her hand stopped. Dadi's face had become red with indignation, and flames leapt from her eyes.

Farhana became alarmed. She was already in awe of Dadi's commanding personality. "What is it, *Ami Jaan*" (Mother dear)? She asked nervously putting the knife down. She had never seen her mother in law in such a furious state.

"Farhana!" Dadi roared again. "What is this I'm seeing? Kanwal has just gone in a car with a strange boy right in front of my eyes. Either you, both husband and wife, have gone blind or you have closed your eyes deliberately. I'm asking you, why have you two slackened your grip so much where Kanwal's concerned? Ever since I've come, I've been troubled at seeing her incorrect ways.

Farhana, who was already at her wit's end with Kanwal's wilful attitude, hearing her mother-in-law's words, folded her arms on the table and putting her forehead on them, burst into tears.

Dadi, who was greatly enraged and was thinking that she would get some answers from Farhana relating to Kanwal's unacceptable behaviour, instead became dumbstruck at seeing her daughter-in-law crying.

"Ami Jaan," Farhana said between sobs. "You don't know how badly distressed I am because of her improper behaviour and ways. She's grown up. We cannot be too harsh in our treatment of her or use force. We can only admonish her, advise her. She turns down every word of mine and Kaleem's as a joke."

"But still, Farhana, to look after your children, to check up on them, to be watchful of them and guard them is the duty of the parents."

Dadi had become a bit appeased at seeing her daughter-in-law's sorrowful face. But still she felt it was her son's and daughter-in-law's fault that Kanwal had turned out this way.

"Ami Jaan," Farhana said instantly, "Don't accuse us for this. You have examples of Hamid and Sunbul in front of you. Haven't we brought them up in an Islamic and Eastern way as well as the Western?"

"When have I said that, Farhana? But you could have explained the vicissitudes of the world to Kanwal. It's the duty of the parents to prevent their children from doing the wrong things."

"Do you think we haven't done that? You have seen for yourself that she doesn't sit with us. She has distanced herself from us. Every time I try to make her understand or advise her to mend her ways, she dashes her foot on the floor and leaves the room. She doesn't listen to us; nor does she do what we say."

Dadi had another objection. "She comes home so late at night. You could phone her and ask her to come home. What's the use of having a mobile phone?"

Farhana sighed in despair. "We've done it all. When does she take our calls or reply to our texts? She responds to none of us—not me, not Kaleem, not even Sunbul or Hamid. Now, all of us have left her the way she is. We used to get tired of ringing her and not being received.

In the end, we just gave up." She blew out a deep breath. "I don't know where I've gone wrong in bringing her up," she said in a choked tone.

Dadi started feeling pity for Farhana. She looked extremely distressed. "If you have made a mistake somewhere, then it has to be rectified too. She has to mend her ways." Dadi looked at Farhana's woebegone face and then, patting her shoulder with compassion, she went out of the kitchen.

At night when Kaleem came home, Dadi, seeing an opportunity, talked decisively with him.

He listened to his mother with his head bowed and then said in a dejected voice, "Ami Jaan, we have tried in every way. She's nearly twenty one. She's an adult. Lawfully, according to this country she's a free person. She has her own independent life. In this country a child becomes independent and is free after sixteen years of age. If we become too severe with her, she'll become rebellious."

He looked very helpless. Dadi's heart became stricken. "Still, my son . . . It's the parent's duty to show their children the right way."

"Do you think we haven't tried doing that or explaining that." He repeated the same words Farhana had said.

Dadi sat dumbfounded, fretting and fuming inside at the powerlessness of her son and daughter-in-law.

Anathema on this society and this country—where mothers and fathers were scared of their own children! In Pakistan, parents administered not only a sharp rebuff but a shoe beating too if necessary, to set the children right and mend their ways.

In her heart, she intended that, today, come what may, she would make Kanwal see her wrongdoings and direct her and put some common sense in her.

It was nearly ten o clock when Kanwal returned home at night. She had the key to the front door. Kaleem and Farhana were in the sitting room watching TV. Kanwal, as usual, habitually called out "Hi" from the passage and, with loud thuds, climbed the stairs and went into her bedroom.

Dadi, after finishing her *Isha Namaz* (night-time prayer) prayed for a long time to God to direct Kanwal to the right path. After invocations, with the rosary in her hand, she went to Kanwal's room.

Kanwal was surprised at seeing Dadi and started wondering about the purpose of Dadi's visit to her room. Before today, Dadi had never come to her room at this time of the night.

She quickly picked up her scattered clothes from the chair and said, "Sit down, Dadi."

Her mobile rang at the same time. Her hand automatically reached out for the mobile. Dadi's eyebrows knitted at Kanwal's movement. Seeing Dadi's irritated look, Kanwal became confused, so did not receive the call. She had some regard for Dadi. The mobile kept on ringing in her hand, but she sat there on the edge of her bed quietly.

For some time, Dadi talked to Kanwal about this and that, and then she brought the object of her visit to her tongue.

"Beti" (daughter), "the boy who came in the car this morning—who was he?"

Kanwal thought in her heart, *Here we go again*, and said, "He was my friend, Dadi."

Her phone was bleeping repeatedly. That meant two or three texts had come together. Kanwal's attention was drawn towards the texts. She was impatient to read them but couldn't do so in the presence of Dadi.

Dadi's eyes were fixed gravely on her. "Friend! Beti, our society, culture, and religion don't permit a girl and boy's friendship."

"Oh, come on, Dadi. Don't be so old-fashioned. These are the things of the past."

Dadi's rosary beads were falling one over another through her fingers. She wasn't an illiterate, country woman. She had passed eight classes of her times, which were more than the eight classes of today. Her heart jolted at Kanwal's words. But she had come, determined to talk to Kanwal no matter what. "It's not about being old-fashioned. We are Asian people, and our Eastern etiquette and cultures demands are something different, which you are exchanging for Western culture."

Another beep came. Dadi looked at Kanwal in vexation. Kanwal glanced quickly at the phone. She was in a hurry to read her texts. She wanted Dadi to go out of her room so she could read her texts. She fidgeted restlessly in her place.

"But, Dadi, I live here in the West, not in a Third World country. If I follow the ways and customs of here, what's so wrong with that? I'm British. When in Rome, do as Romans do."

"You are right to an extent, but, Kanwal, you make the English people's good qualities and virtues your own. Don't make their wrong things your own. If you conform to the West blindly, then you will lose your own recognition and identification."

God! Such a difficult Urdu. Kanwal was getting tired and weary of Dadi's thick Urdu words.

She opened her eyes wide. "What have I done, Dadi?"

"This going around with strange men, is that a good thing?"

"But I've told you; he's my friend."

Dadi's patience was slipping out of her hands, but still she forbore and said, "As I've said before, Islam does not permit this kind of friendship. Beti, heed my word. Don't meet up in alone with strange men. Shaitan" (Satan) "is alive. A human being is very weak in front of him. The limits given in Islam are not without purpose."

Instead of taking Dadi's words seriously, Kanwal burst into laughter. "That Shaitan cannot damage anything of mine. If and when he ever comes near me, I'll give him such a beating that he will run away. Now are you satisfied, Dadi?"

Her mobile started ringing again. Kanwal was desperate for Dadi to go now so that she could attend her call. She glanced at the phone in her hand restlessly.

Dadi felt like beating her own head. *Ya Allah!* (Oh Allah!) *Such a stubborn, impudent girl!*

She stood up, but as she walked out of the room, she gave Kanwal another piece of advice. "Limits . . . boundaries set in Islam are for mankind's own benefits. Shaitaan likes to mislead us. Caution is a good thing. A woman's honour is a very valuable thing. Take care of it."

Kanwal let out a deep breath of relief as Dadi left her room. She raised her eyes to the ceiling. *Thank God she's gone.*

Kanwal was fed up with Dadi and her advices.

She pressed the inbox button impatiently and started reading her texts.

Kanwal was very popular with everyone in her class at university. Laughing, making others laugh, talking, joking, and being mischievous were her favourite pastimes. She was sharp in her studies; even without revising very much, she passed with top numbers. Even her professors praised her intelligence. All the boys and girls in her class liked her.

Red and white-complected, vigorous and robust, tall and stout, blue-eyed Robert fell for Kanwal's Asian and British mingled style. He had taken Kanwal out for tea many times after university, and had openly asked her to move in with him—an offer Kanwal had never taken seriously, always shilly-shallying and laughingly dismissing it. She had, anyhow, always considered Robert as nothing more than a friend.

All the students in their class knew that Robert was very interested in Kanwal, and every now and then, he would invite Kanwal to spend the night with him.

This was not really very strange or shocking. Many boys and girls at their university were living together outside marriage.

One day, Kanwal's best friend, Mary, said to Kanwal, "Kono, don't go around with Robert too much. He says strange things about you to everybody. His intentions aren't good. I don't like the way he talks about you to everyone."

"You are just jealous because he takes interest in me and not you," Kanwal said carelessly, chewing her gum.

"I'm your well-wisher, Kono," Mary said with force in her voice.

"Keep your sympathy and well-wishing to yourself. I don't need it." Kanwal scowled at Mary.

"Don't listen to me then. It's got nothing to do with me." Mary made a face.

"Well, next time, mind your own business." Kanwal glared at her.

"Fine. Don't tell me I didn't warn you." Mary shrugged her shoulders and walked away.

It was some days later, the professor hadn't arrived for one of Kanwal's classes by the time the class was to start, and the room was filled with a hubbub of clamouring students, making noise and entertaining each other. Kanwal was sitting with her group, laughing and talking.

Suddenly, Robert leapt up on the table in front of the class and, putting his hand up, cried out in a loud voice, "Listen. Listen. Today I am asking Kanwal in front of everyone." He looked directly into Kanwal's eyes. "Kanwal, will you spend the night with me tonight?"

The entire class at once fell silent and stared at them. Some of the students' mouths dropped open wide, and some put their hand over their open mouths in astonishment. Some tried to suppress their laughter inside, and some couldn't stop the smiles from spreading across their faces. Some frowned in displeasure at Robert's question, and some simply sat in stunned silence. Some of the students eyes were open so wide they looked like they were about to burst, and some caught their lower lips with their upper teeth. Some muttered "wow" under their breaths, and one or two whistled and said, "Come on, Kono, say yes."

Kanwal found Robert's style extremely unpleasant. She stopped chewing her gum, and her face flushed red with anger. She wanted to claw at Robert's face. He was always talking nonsense like that, but to do so so openly and in such an inappropriate way—what was the need for that? She looked at Robert with hard eyes, and then, filled with rage and glowering at him, she stood up and looked straight at him. She minced out each word. "I'd rather jump into River Thames and end my life than to sleep with you."

With that, shaking with indignation, she swiftly sat back down in her chair, folded her arms, and glared at Robert.

The entire class went into a fit of laughter. Some students shouted loudly, and others whistled. Some gave Robert a thumbs-down, mocking his rejection, while others hooted at him between bursts of laughter. Some clapped feverishly, and some made smirking remarks.

Robert's face became red. He felt insulted and humiliated. It seemed him that everone was laughing at him, taunting him, and making him the butt of their jokes.

He jumped down from the table. "Bitch, I'll get you for this," he muttered under his breath. He said to Kanwal in his heart, *You have insulted me in front of everyone. Almost everything can be forgotten, but not humiliation.*

He couldn't accept rejection. He was determined to soothe his wounded pride.

After her class for the day was over, Kanwal went, as she usually did, to a cafe near her university. Going out with her friends or coming to this cafe after university was almost her daily routine.

Many days had passed since Robert had said those obscene things. She and Robert said "hello" to each other around campus, and she had almost forgotten their tiff that day.

Kanwal drank tea, laughed, and joked, and before she knew it, it had gotten quite late. She got up, and slinging her bag on her shoulder, she said goodbye to her friends and left of the cafe.

Winter was nearly beginning. Darkness spread sooner than usual, but Kanwal wasn't afraid. One or two people were standing at the bus stop waiting for the bus. Most of the shops were almost closed. Only one or two food shops were open. A bus came, but it wasn't Kanwal's. One or two passengers got off the bus, and one or two got on the bus, and the bus moved forward.

Now she was alone at the bus stop. The traffic was coming and going in both directions. The street lights were on. On the opposite corner, a customer was entering a fish and chips shop. Kanwal could see by the in the light of the shop that the serving guy behind the counter was standing attentively, ready to serve the customer.

Kanwal checked the time on her mobile. The bus was taking its time in coming.

She was still standing there waiting when Robert's motorbike stopped in front of her.

Robert took his helmet off and said to Kanwal, "Come on, Kono. I'll drop you home."

Kanwal had been on Robert's motorbike before. She didn't know why, but today her heart was not agreeing to go with him. Perhaps it was because of that day's unpleasantness between them. She said hesitantly. "It's all right. I'll wait for the bus."

"Oh, come on, Kono. I'll take you home." Robert took another helmet out of the motorbike's carrier and held it out to her. Kanwal looked up the road where the bus would be coming from. She saw no sign of the bus.

Robert was looking at her expectantly. She glanced up at the road again. Still no bus. Hesitantly she put the strap of her shoulder bag over her head, adjusted it to the side of her neck on one shoulder and brought it under the other so it hung diagonally across her body leaving her arms free. She took the helmet from Robert's hand with an uncomfortable heart, put it on her head, and sat on the seat behind him.

Robert started the bike, and it moved swiftly along the road. After a while, he turned the bike onto a smaller side street.

Kanwal thought, *Perhaps this is a new shortcut.* She didn't know the streets they were passing through, and they had soon left the main road far behind.

This way was absolutely unfamiliar to Kanwal. The streets were dreary and quiet and desolate.

Kanwal felt uneasy. She shouted at the top of her voice so she could be heard above the wind, "Robert, where are you going? Which way is this?"

"Don't worry, Kanwal. This is a new way." He too screamed out aloud to be heard.

After a while, Robert stopped the bike in a deserted street. Kanwal got off the motorbike, perplexed. Taking her helmet off and holding it in her hand, she asked, "What is it, Robert? Is something wrong with the motorbike?"

Robert got off the motor bike. "The motorbike's fine, but you will surely be defective today," he said menacingly. Depravity was evident on his face.

Kanwal looked around nervously. The street was completely empty. Huge warehouses lined one side of the road, but all the shutters were down and locked at this time of night. On the other side stood buildings whose vacancy was made clear by the wooden boards that barred their windows and doors.

In the dim street light, Robert's face looked frightening.

"Robert, what's this rubbish?" She turned towards him.

"I'll tell you this is, miss holy, chaste Kanwal. You think of yourself as very pure? What did you say? That you didn't want to sleep with me? That you'd rather jump into River Thames and give your life? That's what you said, isn't it? Well, I'll show you right now how holy and chaste you can stay."

A wave of terror penetrated Kanwal's backbone. Mary's words—*Don't go around with Robert too much. His intentions aren't good*—echoed in her mind.

"Robert, take me home right now—this very moment."

"I will take you home. What's the hurry? Come, let's go behind that warehouse." Robert gestured towards a warehouse with his eyes.

"I'm warning you; don't touch me." Kanwal took some steps backwards.

Robert leapt and seized her arm with his hand. He looked wild. "Right then, miss touch-me-not, what did you say? Don't touch you?" Still gripping her arm, he started undoing the buttons of his jacket with his other hand. "Today I will definitely touch you. I will see how you will jump into River Thames and give your life."

Robert's dirty and dangerous intentions became obvious to Kanwal. Certainly, she was a bold and confident girl, born into a free liberal atmosphere and was living in a liberated society. But still, inside, she was that very same ordinary, traditional, timid girl whose honour was dearer to her than life.

She had to get out of here somehow.

The advice that Dadi had given her time and again came to her mind. *H 'é* (sigh) Dadi, she sighed inwardly, *how right you were.*

But this was not the time to remember Dadi's words. This was the time to save herself, not to show cowardice and lose courage.

Her brain was working frantically.

"Look, Robert, don't try to come near me. I . . . I'll make a noise. I'll scream and shout—"

"Go on then." He sneered. "Who's going to hear your screams and shouts?"

A ripple of fear ran through Kanwal's veins. It was true. Who was here?

Kanwal called out to Allah, that great name that easily removes humanity's difficulties, with the veracity of her heart.

"Look, Robert. Someone's coming."

Robert laughed a horrifying laugh. "No one will come here."

He was right. As far as the eye could see, not a soul was in sight.

Kanwal's throat was getting dry, but still she gathered her courage and said, "Robert I'm speaking the truth. Look behind you. Someone is coming."

Robert didn't know what it was in Kanwal's tone, but the hand that was opening his jacket button stopped for a moment. He looked disbelievingly at Kanwal.

"Really, Robert. Someone's coming from behind."

Robert turned his head quickly to look behind him, and for a moment, his grip on Kanwal's arm slackened. And that was the moment Kanwal took advantage of. She hit the helmet, which she was still holding in her hand, on Robert's arm with all her might. An "ooh" came out of Robert's mouth. And her arm was freed from Robert's grasp.

Kanwal ran as fast as she could from there.

Robert swore thickly, climbed on his motorbike, and started it.

Kanwal ran at full speed. She didn't know the area she was in or where these streets might lead. She ran on blindly. She could hear the sound of the motorbike behind her, closing the distance. She had no idea where she was going. Only one thought remained in her mind—she had to save her honour.

All she knew was that she had to escape.

She ran and ran through one street to another. She was panting from running so fast, and her shoes had started pinching her feet. But she didn't stop. She could not stop. To stop would ruination for her. Running was her salvation.

The street lamps were giving out a dim light.

Running into another street, she sensed that it was a residential street and that there were houses here. Should she knock on one of the doors of the houses? No. She didn't have time for that.

The sound of motorbike was getting closer. This street was ending too, and she had no idea where the main road was.

She kept on running and then turned into another street. She was out of breath, and her lungs were nearly bursting under her heaving chest. She had to take some breaths now. She had to inhale air.

Seeing a dark, narrow alley next to a house, she rushed into it. Standing with her back against the wall of the house, she stopped to catch her breath that was blowing out of her like a pair of bellows.

She didn't know how long she stood there gasping for breath. And she didn't know how many more streets she would have to run through. The motorbike's sound was coming nearer. Terrified, she couldn't move from her hiding place.

Dadi's words—*Beti, don't meet strange men in alone. Don't do things that Islam has prohibited*—were hitting her brain like a hammer.

Ya (O) Allah! Save me.

The motorbike passed by. Robert hadn't seen her shaking and standing against the wall of the house in the alley.

She heard the faint muffled sound of her phone ringing in her bag. Without losing any more time, she crept out of the alley, looked up and down the street, and started running again. Her shoes were cutting into her toes, and she was in intense agony. Her feet were in so much pain, but she couldn't lose courage or give up.

And . . . she couldn't run with these shoes anymore. She stopped, took her shoes off, stooped down, and picked them up, and holding them in her hand, she ran barefoot.

And then, all of a sudden, at the end of one street, she came out onto a wide road.

Thank God. She blew out a huge breath.

Stopping, just for a little while and closing her eyes momentarily she bent down and put her hands on her knees and took long deep breaths. Traffic was flowing continuously from both directions.

Still half bent, she turned her neck towards the direction of the coming traffic. She saw a bus coming from far off. At the sight of the bus, she regained her strength. She straightened and reciting Allah's name, ran towards the bus stop. It was a request bus stop. Upon reaching it, she waved her arms like a mad person. *Ya Allah! Let this bus stop. My honour is in your hands. If this bus doesn't stop, then—*

She couldn't think after that. She could hear the faint sound of the motorbike again. She became faint with fear.

The bus pulled up with a slight jerk, and the automatic doors opened. Kanwal threw herself into the bus.

The doors closed.

Kanwal was safe. She had saved her honour. No. Allah had saved her honour.

She could still hear the sound of the motorbike in the distance, or perhaps she was just imagining it. But now Kanwal didn't care. She was in a safe place.

Panting, she held onto the rod in the bus and gasped to get her breath back. Then she felt that the bus driver and the few passengers in the bus were staring at her strangely. She was still holding her shoes in her hand. She was standing barefoot in the bus, and she looked a mess, fatigued and tired.

The bus driver was looking at her inquiringly, his eyebrows raised. He couldn't drive without her paying the fare. He waited patiently as, with her other shaking hand, Kanwal fumbled in her bag and took out her bus pass and touched it on the card reader. The beep sounded and the green light flashed at the same time. The bus driver nodded his head, straightened his face towards the road, and drove the bus off.

Kanwal fell into a seat. Her body was still shaking, and she was perspiring. She put the shoes on the floor of the bus and slipped her aching feet into them.

Tears started flowing from her eyes.

The words that Dadi had spoken to her from time to time were raising a tumult in her heart,

Don't meet men while in alone. Islam does not allow it.

Shaitaan is alive. He misleads. He seeks opportunities to ensnare us in his noose.

Mankind is very weak. He entices him to fall into his traps. The limits set in Islam are for mankind's own benefit. Shaitan wants us to transgress those limits. Don't let him win.

Stay away from Shaitaan's influence.

Understand the real essence of Islamic instructions.

The limits that Islam has defined are not without purpose.

Refrain from the things Islam has prohibited.

Think of you mother and father's teachings.

Set your heart on Islam.

Read Namaz. You will get peace in your heart.

Read the Quran. Your heart will be illuminated.

Follow the Quran. You'll be guided.

Ha'e' (sigh), Dadi, Kanwal thought. *How right you were. How worldly and truthful were all of those things you said.*

Kanwal knew very well that the passengers in the bus were still staring at her strangely, but she had no control over her heart and her tears. She kept remembering her worthy of respect Dadi, whose instructions and guidance she had met with jokes, whose advice she had never paid any attention to.

She was remembering her dearer than life parents from whome she had distanced herself.

She was remembering her dear brother, Hamid, and her sister-in-law, Fatima, of whom she had become so unmindful.

And more than anything she was remembering her lovely, sweet sister Sunbul, whom she had stopped thinking of at all . . . stopped visiting in her home . . . stopped chatting with on the phone . . . stopped having that little chitter chatter with, that was of no use but still seemed very important . . . stopped gossiping about family politics going on within relatives here and in

Pakistan. Through her own negligence and selfishness, she had lost all that sisterly closeness with Sunbul. She never bothered to ask how her brother-in-law, Ahmer, was and she had never taken the time to love her little nephew. She had even neglected him.

All in all, she had neglected everyone.

How sincere were those people and how ignorant and foolish and stubborn she had been in thinking that she could push back from them, from her religion, and from her Asian ways.

She remembered that Dadi had once said, "Make the good things of the West your own. If you copy them blindly, you will lose your own recognition and identity. There's still time. Hold yourself. Be careful. Don't go astray any longer, so that it doesn't happen that you will regret your actions later."

And she remembered, how when she was in primary school, her mother used to take her to the mosque near their home, where Quranic classes were held every day for young children after school time. She would drop her and then pick up her up when the class had finished. This duty, her mother had taken upon herself so that Kanwal could learn Namaz and Quran at a young age–so she could memorize these teachings as they would be like a torch to guide her throughout her life.

And . . . Instead of following that path, that was illuminated by that torch, she was walking towards darkness.

Her religion taught lessons of lightness, and she was going towards obscurity, losing herself in a maze of darkness.

Her religion showed the obvious, and she was going towards oblivion.

Her religion was about improving lives, and she was set on impairing her life.

Islam was a pioneer, and she had chosen to emulate others.

Islam was always there for her—to guide her and show her the way—and she had ignored it, had let herself be misled.

So what if she had been born and brought up here and had been nurtured in this country? She was still a Muslim, wasn't she? A British Asian Muslim. She should have taken pride in that. Why had she forgotten that? Her roots and seed were from Pakistani Muslim parents. Why had she forgotten that?

She didn't know where the bus was going. She startled when the bus driver called out, "This is the last bus stop. The bus doesn't go any farther."

Dadi didn't have a clue what time of night it was.

Kaleem and Farhana had gone to Birmingham to see some relatives.

Hamid and Fatima, as usual, had come after work in the evening to visit Dadi and had gone home.

Sunbul too, as was her daily habit, had phoned to enquire how Dadi was and whether she needed anything.

Dadi had finished reading her Isha Namaz but still hadn't gotten up from her prayer mat. Her heart was fearful. Kanwal was later today than ever before.

Even though she knew Kanwal didn't receive calls from home or reply to the family's texts, she had dialled Kanwal's number to ask where she was and what time she'd be back. The phone had kept on ringing and had then gone to her voice mail.

Many times, she'd thought, alarmed, that she might phone Kaleem and Farhana or Hamid or Sunbul and tell them that Kanwal hadn't come home, but every time she left it. What was the point of disturbing and worrying everyone?

Dadi could do nothing but wait. She couldn't sleep in this state, so she stayed on her prayer mat.

"Ya Allah, show the straight path to this young girl." She was weeping as she prayed.

She was thinking that simply explaining or making Kanwal understand was no longer a solution to this problem. She had to, with full love and pure intentions, try her utmost and do everything possible to bring Kanwal out of this whirlpool she was caught in.

At that very time, tired and ready to fall over from exhaustion, Kanwal, with unsteady hands, opened the front door and let herself inside the house. Relieving her painful feet from her shoes, she crossed the passage and with weary, aching steps, she started climbing the stairs slowly, holding the banister.

At hearing the front door open and then closing from the inside and then Kanwal's footsteps on the stairs, Dadi lifted both of her open hands up in a gesture of thanksgiving to Allah.

Allah, Tera shuker hai (Thank you Allah). She blew out a breath of relief.

But there were no hurried loud thuds that usually announced Kanwal's ascending and descending of the stairs—only the tired heaving and creaking of the stairs.

Dadi's heart became uneasy.

Up on the landing, Kanwal saw that a light was coming from Dadi's room. With unsteady hands, she pushed the already half open door, and with dishevelled haired, swollen eyes, and a precarious balance, Kanwal heaped into Dadi's lap.

Dadi's heart got frightened. *Ya Allah! Khair!* (O Allah! Do well). She put her hand to her heart alarmed at Kanwal's discomposed condition.

"Dadi," Kanwal said between sobs. Her state of mind was in disarray. She looked wild. "I'm speaking the truth. I have come back home the same as I was when I left the house this morning. My body is just as it was when I took off this morning for the university. But mentally and spiritually, I'm shaken from the inside. Really, Dadi, I'm speaking the truth . . . I lost myself for a bit. But Allah is merciful, benevolent, compassionate, and forgiving. He's very kind. He's shown me the straight path in a strange way. Today, he has saved your Kanwal's honour. I was going towards darkness . . ." She looked at Dadi with a tear-stained face. "Take me back to the brightness, Dadi . . . back to the lights. Mum and Dad made me learn Namaz and the Quran at a very young age, so that there would be guidance in my life, leadership in my life. But I've forgotten, Dadi. Teach me to read Namaz and the Quran again, Dadi. Help me refresh what I once knew. Please . . ."

Dadi lifted the weeping and shaking Kanwal's head up with her hands, kissed her tear-drenched face, and recited a verse of the Holy Quran in her tongue. She blew her breath on her face, after invocation, and held Kanwal to her chest.

"Please, bring me back towards the light, Dadi, please . . . Please . . ."

"Insha'Allah, meri bachi" (God willing, my child).

Held in Dadi's warm embrace, Kanwal felt a peace start to descend over her whole body. And putting her head on Dadi's lap and closing her eyes, she laid there restfully.

Kanwal had definitely changed.

She again started memorizing the Namaz, which she had nearly forgotten due to her carelessness. She starting rereading the Quran, at first falteringly, and then, day by day, her reading gathered speed. If she went out, she told everyone in the house. She came straight home from university. If for some reason she got held up and would be late, she phoned home to inform her family. She ate with the household and, in the evening, sat with her family for a while before going upstairs to her bedroom. She even started looking for a part-time job.

This pleasant change in Kanwal affected everyone in the house. Hamid, Fatima, and Sunbul were happy with Kanwal's altered state. Kaleem and Farhana, as well as being relieved and thankful to Allah, were also very grateful to Dadi.

Kanwal had started going back to university after taking some weeks off to gather herself.

She had apologized to Mary for her rudeness when Mary had warned her about Robert. Her university mates had noticed the change in her attitude and made comments about it, to which Kanwal listened, smilingly and laughingly.

Robert had had an accident after that day. He had broken his leg and was now in the hospital for many weeks.

Kanwal went to see him. She had forgiven him and cleared her heart towards him.

At seeing Kanwal, he said, with an embarrassed smile, "I was going out to get revenge on you for insulting and humiliating me, and look what I've done to myself instead. Did you curse me, Kono?"

Kanwal shook her head as she sat in the chair by his bed. "I don't believe in evil maledictions." She placed her bag on her lap and put her hands on it.

"Ooooh!" Robert had moved his plastered leg by mistake as he'd tried to raise the head of his bed with a remote control.

Kanwal looked at him with concern. "Are you all right, Robert?"

"Yeah. I'm fine." It was clear from Robert's face that he was in pain.

He pulled his pillow up a bit in a comfortable position and then, turning his face towards her, said quietly, "I'm sorry for that day, Kono."

"It's all right, Robert," Kanwal said. "I'm not angry with you. Actually, I've come to thank you. If you hadn't done what you did that day, I would have never returned to the right path. Because of your actions, I've come back to my own people and family and have realised the importance of my religion, and I've become inclined towards my religion again. Your wrong actions have shown me what the right actions are. Because of that day I've returned to my real path. I have understood the difference between trueness and imitation. I want to thank you for that. You made it happen."

She lowered her eyes and looked at her hands on the bag.

"That means you can forgive me?"

"Yes, I can forgive you, Robert. Islam says it's good to forgive."

Somehow, Kanwal looked very different to Robert—very fresh, very revived, and very radiant. He looked at her quietly for some time.

Kanwal sat beside the bed for a while, and then she got up, and putting her bag's strap over her shoulder, said, "Okay, I'll be going now."

"Stay a little more," Robert said quickly, as if he didn't want her to go.

"Dadi said I should come home early and also that I shouldn't meet strange men while alone," she said with so much innocence that a spontaneous smile spread across his face.

He laughed light-heartedly. "Then why have you come to meet me here alone?"

"How am I alone? This is a hospital ward. It's a neutral place. There are patients here, visitors here, nurses, doctors, cleaners, and food servers."

"What you want to say is that you are safe here." His tone had a hint of teasing.

"Absolutely safe. Allah's with me, and I know now how to keep myself safe."

Robert went quiet again. After a while, he asked slowly, "Does she know you've come to see me."

"Oh, yes. I told her. Dadi's very broadminded and is in the right to move with the world. As long as I don't transgress the limits my religion has marked. Islam is very considerate. All answers can be found in it. And anyway, in Islam enquiring after a not well person is a virtuous deed." And then she added, tongue in cheek, "So you see, I'll be rewarded."

"Will you see me again?" He was observing her with solemnity.

Kanwal looked at him for a while and then said, "No . . . I don't think so. We'll finish university soon anyway, and no one knows where any of us will be tomorrow."

"We all have each other's numbers and email addresses and know where each other live." God knows what Robert was hoping for?

"Phone numbers and email addresses can be changed or deleted or they can be left there in the contacts lists of names and contacts, never to be used."

"Does that mean you will change your home address too?" Robert teased her. There was a glint in his blue eyes.

A smile came to Kanwal's lips. "But I'm certain you will not come up to my house."

Robert did not reply but only kept on looking silently at her.

"Really, Robert, I have to go now." Kanwal turned to go.

"You couldn't have run faster than the motorbike, Kanwal." Robert's voice behind her back was so low that she had barely heard it.

Kanwal's back stiffened. She swirled around instantly and stared wide-eyed at him.

Robert's gaze was fixed on her, and he looked very serious.

"You mean . . . You mean . . . ?" Bewilderment and uncomprehension filled Kanwal's eyes.

"That day, I wasn't going to do anything bad with you. I couldn't forget your insulting me. I only wanted you to taste the flavour of that experience, of what I felt that day, and teach you a lesson for the insult you hurled upon me. I was just going to frighten you a little and then take you home."

He stopped what he was saying and looked around the ward for a moment and then, fixing his gaze back on her face, said softly, "Do you really think you could have run faster than the motorbike?" He repeated his previous question and then said, "And do you really think I believed you when you said someone was coming from behind?"

He shook his head. "No, Kanwal. When you were running away after hitting my arm with the helmet, I deliberately let you go and deliberately kept the bike's speed slow. And when you ran into that alley, I drove past you, even though I knew you were hiding there. I stopped the bike on another street and walked silently to the end of the street you were on and stood at the side of a house. I stood there until you had, without seeing me, run past and climbed into that bus. I wanted to see you safe. I wanted you to be home safely . . ." His paused, but his expression was steady as he spoke again. "I was just going to scare you a bit, tire you a bit and then take you home." Robert's voice was very quiet.

Kanwal stood there, eyebrows raised in astonishment.

Robert's eyes were stuck on Kanwal's face. He continued in a soft tone. "And then, keeping my bike at a short distance, I followed the bus. Before you got off, I parked the bike in a side street and watched you. I stood there till you went inside your home and didn't leave until you had closed the door. After that, I went on my way too."

Robert went quiet. His eyes hadn't moved from Kanwal's face. She was still looking at him perplexed.

"I swear to God, Kono, it's the honest truth. Believe me."

Suddenly, he looked very truthful to Kanwal. She lowered her eyebrows and said simply, "I believe you, Robert." And then she added, "I have to go now. Dadi will be waiting for me."

"You will meet me again now, won't you?" Robert's voice had hope in it. "I mean . . . not alone . . . in front of everybody, in a neutral place," he quickly clarified. There was a twinkle in his eyes and sprightliness too.

A smile spread involuntarily across Kanwal's lips, and then without answering, she turned around and walked away from the bed towards the exit door of the ward.

Robert watched her go silently.

Kanwal reached the exit door. She put her hands on the door to push it open. She wanted to go straight out, but without knowing why, she hesitated, turned her head, and looked back towards the ward.

Robert, with his face turned towards her, was watching her. Kanwal's hand lingered on the door for a moment.

Whatever it was, because of him she had come out of obscurity and had returned to her real path.

Because of him, her heart had changed and had turned towards Allah.

Because of him, she had escaped from more anonymous wandering about, more being misled. When a person is occupied somewhere else and is on the verge of forgetting Allah, then Allah causes something to happen that will make that person feel His presence.

Robert, to give her a taste of the degradation he had experienced through her hand, to teach her a lesson, had done all that.

And so had Allah; to cause her to taste the flavour of suffering through Robert's hands, to teach her a lesson and to bring her back on the rightful way, to bring her back towards him, had made Robert do all that.

Robert was looking at her with a request in his clear blue eyes.

Kanwal moved her eyes away and then, turning her back, pushed the door open and walked out of the ward.

Allaha had become successful!

Allah had always been successful!

And Allah would always be successful!

Today was the day Dadi was going back. Kanwal's mind was in turmoil.

The whole family had come to the airport to see Dadi off.

Kanwal hugged Dadi. "Please don't go, Dadi."

Dadi enfolded Kanwal in her arms. "Beta, I won't stay here anymore. But, yes, you must come to me."

"That I will. But what's wrong with you staying here?"

"There's nothing wrong in staying here, beta, but everybody wants to go back to their real base because that's their identity and their recognition."

She kissed the top of Kanwal's head.

"I'll wait for you, beta."

Then after embracing everyone, she joined the queue to have her hand luggage checked in and to go into the departure lounge, where after some time, the plane going to Pakistan would be ready to take passengers to the land of Pakistan.

History

When I had my hair cut short, my mother-in-law said that not only had I sinned but I had also lost my Eastern pride and beauty.

When I plucked my eyebrows or bleached my face, my mother-in-law said that it was a sure sign that I would be going straight to hell.

When I wore clothes with matching shoes, jewellery, or make-up, my mother-in-law said that these were all indications of the world coming to an end, and Allah was going to throw me into the fire of hell to be burned.

When I made myself look pretty in the evening for my husband just before he came back from work, my mother-in-law said that this was the way to keep my husband dancing around my little finger and that I knew how to trap and please men.

When I invited my friends to tea and laughed and joked with them, my mother-in-law said that, after so much laughter, tears always followed. Some sort of grief and sorrow would befall me, and I would be weeping soon.

When I broke a cup accidently, my mother-in-law said that I was only here in her house to ruin and destroy her valuables, which she had saved and skimped to buy. And what had my parents given me on my wedding? Just a little dowry, and things of such a cheap quality that she was ashamed to show them to her relatives, friends, acquaintances, and neighbours.

When I washed clothes, my mother-in-law said that I didn't know how to scrub the collars clean. What had my mother taught me? Nothing but to argue and quarrel. That I could do with expertise.

When I cooked something, my mother-in-law said that it was too greasy, too salty, too spicy, too sweet, overcooked, under cooked . . .

When I answered her back, my mother-in-law said that I had a long tongue as sharp as a knife, like my mother.

How I wish I could cut her with that knife.

And so on and on it went. I was sick and tired of her.

I said to my husband, "I hate your mother. She makes me sick. She doesn't like anything I do. She's always finding faults with me. If I could, I would kill her."

My husband looked at me coldly. "How would you like to kill her? Poison her, strangle her, drown her, stab her, set fire to her, shoot her, push her from the rooftop, throw her under a train, have a car run over her, suffocate her, murder her yourself? Or would you like me to hire someone to murder her? There are many ways of killing. Please choose which one you like best."

I glared at my husband. I could have happily killed him too.

The next morning, my husband said to my mother-in-law, "Mother, what is all this? You are always going on at Shazia. You are always finding faults with her. Can't she do anything right in your eyes?"

My mother-in-law glared at me first and then at my husband. She could have happily killed him too.

"So," she said, "she does have you dancing around her finger. You are like a puppet. She pulls your strings. What is the world coming to? Sons speaking like this to their mothers, and all in favour of their wives."

She started wailing.

My husband gave her a disgusted look and left for work.

I smiled triumphantly. She saw me smiling. If looks could have killed, I would have been dead by now.

"So"—she narrowed her eyes and flared her nostrils—"you've been telling tales about me, trying to turn my son against me. I hope you are satisfied, you bitch."

I had my hands on my hips now. "I am. And bitch yourself."

"What," she raged. "Calling me names. How dare you?"

Blazing from head to foot, she flew towards me and slapped me on the face. How I hated this woman, my mother-in-law. I wasn't going to stand for that. I had to get even. I slapped her right back. There! Tit for tat! She stared at me in disbelief. Then she screamed and, still screaming, ran out of the house into the front garden. I raced after her.

"People," she shrieked out to the neighbours, turning her face from one side to the other. Heads started popping from doors and windows. "People, come and see the cruelties of this woman." She shook a finger at me. "She has just slapped me."

She was in such a rage she could hardly speak. Spit had gathered at the corner of her mouth.

Neighbours were coming out now. Some stood leaning by their front garden walls to look. Some watched from their windows. Some hovered in their doorways. Some rushed out of their houses to where we were. They were used to us brawling, but they always enjoyed these feuds as if it was the first time.

It was a typical Asian street in an Asian-filled area in England, where everybody liked to know everybody's business and everybody butted into everybody's business, making it their business, and gave free advice and suggestions. These broils were a source of amusement to them, like a drama.

We had other spectators too. Passersby and onlookers joined the neighbours. They all stood around us in amusement, watching mother-in-law and daughter-in-law in combat.

My mother-in-law wailed and lamented about me.

I raged about my misfortune to be married into her house.

My mother-in-law's sympathizers (mostly mothers-in-law from the neighbourhood) stood beside my mother-in-law like an army and tried to comfort her.

My sympathizers (mostly daughters-in-law from the neighbourhood) took their place by me and tried to console me.

We had fought before, my mother-in-law and I, but never like this, so openly, so verbally and physically abusive to each other.

Now, on one side, it was her. On one side, it was me, and we opened fire, accusing each other. I cried out, "You don't have a daughter. That's why you don't know how to treat me like one."

"If there are daughters like you, then I'm glad I never had one," she cried back and tried to free herself from the clutches of her sympathizers, ready to attack me.

"Uh-ha!" I tried to loosen my sympathisers' grasp, ready to lunge at her.

More abuses and accusations followed.

"You are always finding faults with everything I do."

"You don't do anything right. You deliberately irritate me."

"You have never accepted me as you daughter-in-law."

"You have never tried to be like one."

"You are jealous of me."

"Jealous of you, my foot."

"You should have married your son yourself."

My mother-in-law turned to her army with fake tears in her eyes. "See. See her. What a black tongue she has."

"And you have a poisonous one. Like a snake."

My mother-in-law shed some more crocodile tears.

"I regret the day I chose her for my son. I made such a bad mistake," she bemoaned in self-pity.

"And I regret the day fate led your footsteps into my parents' house for my *rishta*" (match). I blighted my fate.

My mother-in-law spread her *dupatta* (long scarf or stole) and started cursing me. A voice from my mother-in-law's side came. "Oh, she's fainted. She's passed out. Her daughter-in-law gives her too much grief. Get the water. Quick. Someone."

I tried to peer through my mother-in-law's sympathizers. They were holding her by the arms. Her eyes were closed. Dead, I hoped. Someone was sprinkling water on her. She came back to life. That was quick.

"*Oonh!*" I tossed my head. "Acting. Fraud," I told my sympathizers.

My mother-in-law was ready to take position again. We started firing.

"Malicious."

"Wicked."

"Mentally disturbed."

"Lunatic. You should be locked up."

"You sicken me."

"You are loathsome."

"You are a loose woman."

"I know, too, what you used to do in your youth."

"Shut your mouth up, you daughter of a bitch."

"Ah ha! Truth pricked you like a needle, did it, daughter of a dog?"

"Revolting."

"Repelling."

"Two-faced."

"Hypocrite."

"I can't stand the sight of you."

"I don't want to look at you either."

"Foul-mouthed."

"Gross."

"As if I don't know that you go to sorcerers to do black magic on me."

"I know, too, that you go to necromancers to have evil amulets made to cast evil spells on me."

"You will not have dominion over me."

"I won't let you have authority over me either."

"I hope to God there'll be insects in your grave."

"I hope scorpions will eat your dead body."

"Dear Allah, let no one have a daughter-in-law like mine. Give her a son. Let her be a mother-in-law too."

My mother-in-law spread out her dupatta and raised her eyes to the sky.

"I will never be a mother-in-law like you," I vowed in front of everyone.

My mother-in-law said, "I'll leave this house and never come back."

Her sympathizers calmed her. "You have worked and toiled for this house all your life. If you go, she'll inherit everything."

My mother-in-law calmed down. She wasn't going anywhere anyway.

I said, "It's all right. I'll go. She's welcome to this house."

"Don't say that. This is your house too. You have as much right to live in it as her," my sympathizers advised me.

I took their advice. I wasn't going anywhere anyway.

We were utterly exhausted. It had to end now. Before the final round, I wanted the final word. I'd make sure of that. "Wait till your son comes home tonight. He will have to make a choice. Either me or you."

I shrugged off my sympathizers, who were trying to comfort me. I ran into my bedroom and slammed the door shut. I felt victorious. I'd had the final word. Or had I?

I heard my mother-in-law yell, "Yes, let him come home tonight. He will decide. You or me?"

A few minutes later, I heard her door slam.

My husband came back from work. First, he went to his mother.

"Go," she shouted. "Go to that crafty, cunning, treacherous wife of yours. Go and please her."

My husband came into our bedroom.

"Go to that hateful, spiteful, vicious mother of yours. That woman has made my life miserable."

My mother-in-law had followed her son and now stood in our doorway. "I have made your life miserable? You home wrecker. You're the one who's ruined a happy home."

"You're the one who has destroyed my life."

My husband shouted, "Be quiet, both of you."

I said, "You have to make a choice. Keep one of us. It's either her or me."

"Let her go," my mother-in-law implored her son. "I will find you a better and more dutiful wife—one who will make you happy."

My husband looked at me. I managed to squeeze some tears from my eyes and let out a heartrending sob from my lips.

He looked at his mother. She managed a pleading look in her eyes and a pitiable expression on her face.

He put his hands on his ears as if in pain. "You both stay. I will be the one who will leave."

He walked out of the room, and moments later, we heard the front door slam.

My mother-in-law gave me an evil look and went back to her room.

I thought, *Oh! Where can he go? He'll be back.*

But he didn't come back, and I found out I was pregnant.

We never saw my husband again, but we did hear that he had married an orphan girl from an orphanage and was living a quiet, peaceful life somewhere in the world.

My son said to me, "Mother, what have you got against Razia? She can't do anything to please you. You are always finding faults with her."

I looked at Razia, my daughter-in-law. She had a smug look on her face.

"You," I minced out the words. I would have liked to mince her too. "You troublemaker. This house has never had a moment of peace since you've entered it."

"Oh, before I came, it was heaven, wasn't it?" she replied sarcastically.

"Yes, it was. You turned it into hell."

"You are a fine one to talk. We all know what kind of heaven it was. You made it a burning hell for your mother-in-law. That poor woman died cursing you." She was ready to open my history book.

"Keep your mouth shut, you silly stupid woman. You are the one who's making this house a burning hell for me."

Accusations and abuses kept flying. My son stood there helplessly.

"Your wife's such a foul-mouthed woman. Are you going to stand there and watch her insulting me? Look at the way she uses her tongue. Have you ever heard or seen such a poisonous tongue before?"

"And you have a snake where your tongue should be," my daughter-in-law shrieked.

My son pushed her into the bedroom. I felt a rush of warmth towards him. After all, he was my son. I had given birth to him. Of course, he was not going to let that woman disrespect me.

"Come here a minute, Mother," he beckoned, standing near the room. I went lovingly to him, but he pushed me inside the room too and quickly locked the room from outside.

"You two can stay in there and sort out whatever it is between you two. I'll see you in the evening," he called out and went to work.

In the room, I gave my daughter-in-law a murderous look. She gave me an equally murderous look back.

I slumped in a chair with a thud. She sat on the edge of the bed with a thud. I made faces at her. She scowled and poked her tongue at me. I spat on the floor. She spat on the floor. I looked out of the window. She stared at the wall. I bit my nails. She scratched her toes. I read. She slept.

In the evening, my son opened the door.

"I hope you two have come to your senses."

My daughter-in-law screamed, "You have to make a choice this very minute. Keep your mother or keep your wife."

I looked at my son hopefully. "Let her go, son. I'll marry you off again. I'll choose a better and more beautiful wife."

My son said in an exasperated tone, "Mother, marriages are not vegetables. You can't just throw them away like rotten carrots and potatoes."

"Her or me?" screamed my daughter-in-law.

He looked from one to the other. "Don't make me choose. I want to keep both of you," he said quietly.

"Well, I'm not going to stay with her." My daughter-in-law pointed towards me. "You are welcome to her. I'm leaving."

She went into her bedroom, packed a suitcase, and left. My son watched his wife leaving.

Good riddance, I thought. *I hope he doesn't go after her.*

He had read my thoughts. "Don't worry, Mother. I'm not going after her," he said sadly. "But," he continued, "I'm not going to stay here either." He looked at my open mouth. "I think I'll follow my father's footsteps. Goodbye."

History had repeated itself once again.

I was alone now. I had lost my husband, and now I had lost my son too. As I stood in the empty house, I wondered if my daughter-in-law was pregnant. I hoped she was.

GAMBLE

My daughter and I were having a discussion that was gradually leading into an argument. I don't know how this subject had cropped up in our normal everyday conversation, but somehow we had ended up talking about arranged marriages.

My daughter was all in for love marriages, while I was all in favour for arranged marriages. She was very amiable, polite, and well mannered. She pointed out all the good benefits, qualities, and advantages of love marriages, while I pointed out all the good qualities, benefits, and advantages of arranged marriages.

I said, "Arranged marriages work out better. The children, son or daughter, don't have to do the worrying. The parents do all the worrying instead. They are wiser and know what's best for their children."

"Not all the time. Look what happened to Aunty Salma," my daughter reminded me.

(Salma was my cousin. Her husband had divorced her on the very first night of their wedding, after seeing her for the first time. He had said that he didn't find her attractive. He had been told she was very beautiful, but she wasn't in accordance with his expectations.)

"True," I said. "In some cases, mistakes are made by parents in choosing the right person."

"There," said my daughter triumphantly. "In love marriages, you get to know the person really well. It's easier for you to get along well with them after you are married. You know their likes and dislikes. You can handle a marriage easier that way."

I looked at her. How naive she was. Didn't she know marriages were never easy? Arranged or love.

I said, "In love marriages, if you make the wrong choice, you have only yourself to blame." I maintained my stand.

"Are you saying that, in arranged marriages, we could put all the blame on parents if they go wrong?" she asked.

"No," I said. "What I'm saying is that, in love marriages, sometimes you have no one to turn to. Couples can make hasty decisions, like separation or divorce and the like, while in arranged marriages, your elders will come between you if there's a problem. They can consult both of you and will try to put matters right, using their own judgement. They try and usually succeed in keeping the couple together."

"But when you love someone, you love them in spite of their faults and habits," my daughter said, insisted.

"In long-term relations, faults and habits become irritations, even for lovers, and they can lead to a disastrous marriage."

"You are really trying to put me off, aren't you Mum?" she accused

"Not at all," I said. "With arranged marriages, almost everyone gets the chance to get married, usually at the right age, while with love marriages, it can sometimes take you a lifetime to find the person you love, and even then, you are not sure whether he's the right one."

I had her attention, so I continued, "With arranged marriages, even the ordinary ones or plain-looking ones get an equal chance of getting married as the good looking ones. I personally know many plain-looking persons who are leading very successful married lives. In love, a person is easily impressed by the outer beauty rather than the inner beauty."

She wouldn't budge. "I still think children have a right to love a person before they marry them," she persisted.

"I won't disagree with you on that, but love can come after a marriage too," I stressed.

"Oh, don't be silly, Mum. How can someone love a complete stranger? A stranger you meet for the first time on your wedding night? That's ridiculous."

"Well. It's not impossible."

She gave me a queer look and asked, "Do you love Daddy?"

I hesitated, thought, and then said, "Before I answer that, tell me something. Have you found someone you love? Someone you want to marry?"

She went bright red and stood up. "How can you talk like that to your own daughter? You should be ashamed of yourself."

"What is there to be ashamed of? You prefer love marriages. To have a love marriage, you need to find the person you love. All I'm asking is, have you found him?"

She gave me a look that was a mixture of disgust and embarrassment and then went out, slamming the door behind her.

Exasperated, I rolled my eyes to the ceiling. There she was one minute, talking as if she was an expert on the subject, and when I ask her something, she goes of in a huff. So much for her advancement!

She was an easily embarrassed person, my daughter. It was a wonder she was speaking so openly on this subject. Though born and bred in England, she was brought up as a typical Asian female, who started trembling even if a boy said hello to her. She was shy and reserved. I don't know where she got this trait from. Perhaps she had inherited it from my husband's side of the family. She was not very bold and lacked confidence where boys were concerned. How was she going to find a husband in this fast-moving age?

She was nearly twenty. In a year or two, I would like to see her settled. In my opinion, the right marriageable age was between twenty and twenty-five (twenty-two and twenty-three being the ideal age in my view) for girls and twenty-seven and twenty-eight for boys. Of course, that wasn't necessarily a limit. It didn't apply to everyone. It was just my own way of thinking. I believed that girls in that age range found it easier to adjust to their in-laws ways and customs, household duties, and responsibilities of practical life and bearing children.

That night, I told my husband about our discussion.

"Leave her alone," he said. "She's only young. She'll come to her senses as she grows older." He turned his back to sleep. I lay wide awake and thought, *Will she? Did I?*

When I told my friends at college my marriage had been arranged in Pakistan, they stared at me in disbelief. I had just turned sixteen.

Carol shrieked, "At this age and in this society!"

Ruth exclaimed, "In these times and in this country!"

Mary uttered, "You must be mad!"

Susan staggered. "I don't believe it. You are lying!"

Jill advised, "You can get help. Go to the marriage advice people!"

Wendy offered, "I'll go with you!"

Joan urged, "Stand up for yourself!"

Lillian reasoned, "Surely, you don't want an arranged marriage."

Bev observed, "What a stupid old-fashioned way of getting married!"

Sally revolted, "Oh my God, it's disgusting. Marrying a complete stranger!"

Meg shuddered. "Aren't you afraid?"

Norma wondered, "Are you really going through with it?"

And my best friend, Bina, said, "Rani, you can't let them do this to you."

I looked at her.

"You'll go through the same circumstances."

"Never," she said vehemently. "I'll never have an arranged marriage. I'll fight for my rights. No one can force me. I will not be emotionally blackmailed by my parents as you have been. You'll see. You just wait and see, Rani. I'll show you."

I looked sadly at her. She was one of us. Arranged marriages were in our blood, in our culture, in our life. If we wanted to get out of them, we'd have had to bear the consequences.

She turned towards me. "Anyway, what about Amer?"

I averted my face. "What about him?" I lowered my eyes.

"As far as I know, you two—"

I cut her off. "There weren't any promises."

I could feel her looking hard at me. I bowed my head. A tear fell on the floor.

In time, I lost touch with most of my friends, but I did know:

That Carol, my simple friend, had had three children, all by different men who didn't want to settle down.

That Joan, my straightforward friend, after unsuccessfully trying to find a right person, was having an affair with a married man.

That Susan, my plain homely friend, had married and her husband had left her with four children after fifteen years of marriage.

That Sally, my intellectual brilliant friend, had finally decided to settle down at the age of forty with an illiterate bricklayer.

That Wendy, my beautiful model-like friend who had declared that she would get married at the age of twenty, was still single.

That Bina, my dear best friend, was leading a life of great misery with her educated but uncouth in-laws and husband. Her parents had made a bad mistake in choosing her husband. He was a lazy good-for-nothing person, who didn't hesitate to raise his hand against her. Bina worked and laboured for her children.

As I lay beside my husband I thought that maybe I was luckier than most. I had a house, children, and financial security. I was cosy and settled. What more could I want? Then I remembered my daughter's question. Did I love my husband? Where was love though? There was no answer.

The next morning, I was in the kitchen drinking my tea when my daughter walked in shamefaced.

"Sorry about yesterday, Mum. I got carried away." She sat down.

"Never mind." I patted her hand. She was so innocent and beautiful. "It's not your fault. You feel more intense about these subjects at your age."

As I poured out the tea for her, I said to myself, *Who knows? Who can say which marriages are better—arranged ones or love ones? There was a risk in both. When you got married, you took a gamble. Some lost. Some won.*

Lightning Source UK Ltd.
Milton Keynes UK
UKOW02f1054261016
286179UK00001B/3/P